D1248929

DAUGHTERS OF THE MOON

the final eclipse

13

LYNNE EWING

HYPERION/NEW YORK

Also in the
DAUGHTERS OF THE MOON
series:

Copyright © 2007 by Lynne Ewing

First Edition
1 3 5 7 9 10 8 6 4 2
Printed in the United States of America

Reinforced binding

Library of Congress Cataloging-in-Publication Data on file

ISBN-13: 978-1-4231-0843-6
ISBN-10: 1-4231-0843-4

Visit www.hyperionteens.com

This book is for all the wonderful readers of the Daughters of the Moon series who insisted that another book be written. Thank you for all of your letters, e-mails, petitions, phone calls, and Web sites. I am so happy that you have enjoyed reading the books as much as I have enjoyed writing them. I love you all. *Vos estis deae, filiae lunae.* You are goddesses, Daughters of the Moon.

And for all you guys who got behind the movement, demanding another book— I love you, too. Thank you.

The Daughters of the Moon series wouldn't have been possible without the terrific editors who worked on the series. Hugs and kisses to the three of you, Alessandra Balzer, David Cashion, and Jennifer Besser.

In ancient times, during a full moon's night, people gathered outside, and, beneath the lunar glow, they spoke of their dreams and wishes for the future. Selene, the goddess of the moon, looked down and blessed the gatherings. When life grew hard and everyone became discouraged, Selene showered the world with her infinite love. People breathed in her silver moonbeams and were once again filled with joy, their hope restored.

The Moirai, those three sisters of Fate, watched this with growing jealousy. People should be trying to appease them, not dancing in Selene's moonlight. How could anyone remain hopeful in the midst of the floods and famines that the three sisters had woven into the tapestry of life? Outraged, the Fates spun plague, war, and devastating earthquakes into the future. But when those misfortunes struck, instead of bowing to the Fates, more than ever, people sought the light of Selene's hope-giving moon.

The sisters' envy grew until finally, maliciously, they spun unthinkable suffering into the life of one of Selene's favorite Daughters, Penelope.

And so it came to pass that when Penelope fell in love, an ancient evil called the Atrox stole her betrothed and transformed him into a demon. Heartbroken, Penelope pleaded with Selene to let her live to see the Atrox destroyed. But before the goddess could answer, the Atrox granted Penelope's wish. In her haste, Penelope had failed to ask for everlasting youth. With that mistake, she had condemned herself to age forever.

Selene wept. Her sorrow delighted the Fates. Their laughter echoed out past the stars and into the heavens. But they had underestimated Selene's love for her Daughters. The goddess gave Penelope an elixir to stop her aging. In that simple act, she unraveled the threads the Fates had woven and changed Penelope's future.

No one had ever before defied the Moirai. Their powers

were beyond the gods, their decrees immutable; even the great god Zeus bowed to them. The sisters needed revenge—something to pierce Selene's heart. And then the Atrox came to them with a simple request. A young Follower named Stanton had brought a girl from the future back into the past. The Atrox had, thus, been able to witness the girl's bravery before she was even born. It begged the Fates to entwine the girl's destiny with its own so that it might have her.

The Fates agreed, and even though the girl would not be born for centuries, they began spinning the threads they would need to weave the horrible future the Atrox wanted for the yet unborn goddess, a Daughter of the Moon named Vanessa.

CHAPTER ONE

VANESSA LEANED OUT the window and looked up, straining her neck. The clear, boundless sky made her shudder. "Where are the shadows?" she asked. "It's almost nightfall. I know they're awake." She scanned the street below. Heat rose off the pavement, but no dark apparitions rippled in and out of the houses. She felt suddenly afraid. This had never happened before.

"Maybe everyone is inside preparing for a celebration," Serena said from the bed. She refused to look out the windows anymore. "I suppose *they* have holidays, but the quiet . . ."

". . . Is a nice change," Vanessa finished calmly, even though she was screaming with panic inside her own head. She didn't want to alarm Serena yet.

"Maybe they're getting ready to kill us," Serena said.

The resignation in her voice worried Vanessa. She left the window and walked over to the bed. Serena was bone-thin, her eyes joyless, exhausted, and bruised. A week ago, she had started screaming in her sleep, and Vanessa could no longer awaken her from the nightmares.

"Don't leave me," Vanessa whispered through the tightness in her throat. She refused to cry and upset Serena. Her eyes itched and burned from all the tears she had shed so far, and what good had it done?

"I can't go on," Serena said. "Every noise makes me jump, because I think they're coming for us, and then they don't. Maybe that's worse— when they don't. I can't stand the waiting. I just want them to get it over with."

"We'll escape. I promise. I know we will." Vanessa sat on the edge of the bed.

"Don't lie to me." Serena sank back into the pillows. "I know we won't survive as we are now. I just hope I won't remember who I was."

Like Serena, Vanessa could feel the evil growing inside her, the change so subtle she wasn't even sure when it had begun. But she knew she was no longer the person she had been when she, Catty, and Serena had tried to rescue Tianna. She wondered when the darkness would finally become stronger than her will to hold it back.

"It's my fault," Vanessa said at last. "I'm sorry."

"We all thought rescuing Tianna was the right thing to do," Serena countered.

An ancient evil called the Atrox had kidnapped Vanessa, Serena, and Catty and held them hostage until Tianna surrendered to it. But when the Atrox let them go, Vanessa had, instead of fleeing, convinced Serena and Catty to stay and free Tianna. That had been a terrible mistake.

During the struggle, Catty had disappeared. As the Destroyer, she had been destined one day to fight the Atrox alone, and because of that, she had also been its greatest threat. Vanessa knew her best friend was dead.

"All of it's my fault," Vanessa whispered again.

Serena leaned forward and stroked Vanessa's hair. She started to say something, but cursed instead. She pulled back abruptly and stiffened, her eyes wild, darting back and forth, as if she were searching for a place to hide. "They're coming," she said.

Then Vanessa felt the uncomfortable heaviness in the air. A Regulator was near.

Boots thumped on the carpet outside their door. A key turned in the lock, and the Regulator pushed into their room. He carried a silver tea set on a tray. Porcelain cups clattered against each other.

Regulators worked for the Atrox and carried

out its orders. Over time, exposure to its evil, like a chemical reaction, destroyed their bodies. This one looked grotesquely misshapen. Each feature in his face appeared to have melted over the next. Wiry black hairs grew from his flattened nostrils, and he made snorting noises when he breathed. Gray-green scaly skin covered one side of his head and his right arm. He had the ability to disguise his appearance and look male-model gorgeous, but, while they were in Nefandus, Regulators rarely bothered, because their ugliness inspired fear and made it easier for them to police the world in which the Atrox reigned.

"Ugh!" Serena pulled the covers over her head and curled into a ball. "The Atrox gave us the ability to see so we'd have to look at these monsters," she complained, trying to sound gruff, but Vanessa could hear the tremor of fear in her voice.

Without a talisman or a guide to help them, people who weren't residents saw only churning mists. It was one last obstacle to keep Nefandus a secret in case someone accidentally stumbled through one of the portals. Still, Vanessa felt grateful to be able to see. Vision gave her a better chance to escape.

The Regulator began humming as he busied himself preparing their afternoon tea. He offered Vanessa a plate of ginger snaps, his hand lingering on hers. His touch made her wince. She turned away; even so, she could feel him watching her. The sheer fabric of her dress clung to her body and made her feel naked, but she had nothing else to wear.

She clutched the amulet hanging around her neck and studied the face of the moon etched in the metal. The charm had been given to her at birth. Serena wore one, too. Back home in Los Angeles their amulets glowed when Followers were near, but in Nefandus the charms remained still and cold, their magic burned out.

"Tu es dea, filia lunae," Vanessa whispered, trying to calm herself. "You're a goddess, a Daughter of the Moon." But the words only reminded her that she had failed. Her mentor, Maggie, had explained that in ancient times, when Pandora's

box was opened, countless evils and sorrows were released into the world. The last thing to leave the box was hope, the sole comfort for people during hard times. Only Selene, the goddess of the moon, saw the demon sent by the Atrox to devour hope. She stopped the creature, and then took pity on humankind and gave her Daughters as guardian angels, to fight the Atrox and safeguard hope. Vanessa and Serena were two of those Daughters.

The last two, Vanessa thought sadly.

The Regulator gave her a cup of tea. The fragrance of jasmine mingled with his foul breath. The smell made her stomach quiver. She pushed his hand away.

He set the tea and cookies on a table, then left the room, closing the door behind him.

Vanessa waited for the clank of the dead bolt. The sound always made her cringe, but it didn't come this time. She sat up straighter, alert, and listened intently.

Serena threw back her covers and stared at Vanessa. "Is he playing with us, or did he really forget to lock us in?"

"I don't know." Vanessa ran to the door and pressed her ear against the wood. She expected to hear the Regulator snickering on the other side, but all was quiet. She looked back at Serena. "I think he forgot."

"Open the door," Serena said anxiously.

Vanessa took a deep breath, gripped the handle, and opened the door a crack. She peered out. "No one's guarding us."

"Are you sure?" Serena crowded against her. "Did you check for shadows?"

Vanessa understood Serena's fear. Regulators and some Followers could turn into shadows and blend with the dark. The shape-shifters were powerful and dangerous. They could read minds, manipulate thoughts, and even imprison people in their memories.

"It's too bright," Vanessa answered giddily, a foolish grin growing on her face.

Hundreds of candle flames glinted in chandeliers and filled the hallway with dazzling light. No raven black phantoms could have slithered around without being seen.

Serena looked out. "We'd see them for sure," she said, and then she asked, "Do we dare?"

In reply, Vanessa ventured into the hallway. She felt dizzy with excitement and fear. "Which way should we go?"

"The stairs." Serena pointed.

"We'll be too exposed," Vanessa argued. "Anyone walking by will see us."

"Then use your power," Serena urged.

Vanessa had a gift. All the Daughters had one. She could become invisible. She relaxed her body and willed herself to dematerialize—but her molecules remained firmly attached to one another.

"I can't," Vanessa said at last. She hadn't been able to use her ability in Nefandus.

"Let's go." Serena stepped boldly forward.

They crept down the marble staircase without making a sound. Giant mirrors decorated the walls and reflected back a dozen images of their thin, terrified faces.

When they reached the entrance hall, footsteps echoed down another corridor. The noise grew louder with each step.

"It was just another game after all," Serena said miserably, "to give us hope and then take it away. Over and over again they do this to us."

"They haven't caught us yet." Vanessa pulled Serena to an ornately carved door and opened it.

Light from the hallway fell across a landing and below it, across wooden stairs that led down to a dank, dirty cellar.

"It stinks," Serena whispered as she stepped inside. She clenched the handrail and turned ashen. "What's down there?"

Vanessa crowded in next to her and quietly closed the door. A vile stench wafted over her and made her eyes sting. She blinked and waited, listening to the person walking down the corridor.

As the person approached the other side of the door, Vanessa was seized with a sudden need to get away. She acted before she thought, and, taking Serena's hand, eased on to the first step. Her weight made the wood creak. She froze, too terrified to breathe.

"Is someone there?" a haughty, nasal voice called from the entrance hall. And then, after a silence, the voice asked, "Do I sense two sweet goddesses hiding from me?"

Followers fed on fear, and Vanessa could feel this one savoring her terror. His aura seeped under the door and pulsed around her. She swallowed hard to keep from crying out. Serena whimpered beside her.

The door started to open, letting light into the cellar. Vanessa closed her eyes. She didn't want to see his face.

"What are you doing here?" another voice, different from the first one, demanded.

The sound of the door slamming startled Vanessa. She opened her eyes and found herself in complete darkness again. She straightened up, surprised. Serena fell against her, trembling violently, her breathing shallow and fast, but she didn't cry out or utter a sound this time. Vanessa tensed and waited to see what would happen next.

Finally, the nasal voice answered. "I was only admiring the artwork."

"Then why were you opening the cellar

door?" the second voice asked. "That area is forbidden."

"Of course; it was foolish of me to forget
that the Atrox has become suspicious and afraid,"
the nasal voice sneered, and then the tone changed
to one that was servile and flattering. "I must
apologize. I was bored waiting for the other
members of the Cincti to arrive. I suppose I did
meander into restricted rooms."

"Come with me," the other voice ordered.

The two walked away.

"That was Stanton," Serena whispered. "The
second voice belonged to him."

"Are you sure?" Vanessa asked as she stepped
back to the door.

"Of course I'm sure," Serena answered. "I'd
know his voice anywhere."

As hard as the captivity had been on Vanessa,
it had been harder on Serena. She had been in love
with a Follower named Stanton. Their relation-
ship had been forbidden until he became the
Prince of Night, and then nothing was denied
him. But even though his visits would have been

allowed, he hadn't come to see Serena since she had been imprisoned.

"How could Stanton forget me so easily unless everything he told me was a lie?" Serena asked.

Vanessa could hear the pain in her voice. "He's a Follower," Vanessa reminded her. She wrapped her fingers around the doorknob, anxious to leave. It didn't turn. "We're locked in."

"That can't be." Serena nudged Vanessa aside and tried the door. The latch rattled, but didn't click open. "Did the creepy one lock us in?"

"It doesn't matter," Vanessa said with determination. She started down the stairs. "We'll find another way out."

Serena didn't follow her. "We don't know what's down there. The cellar could go on forever. And it stinks—something foul must live down there."

Vanessa paused. "We can't wait here. That Follower will come back. He sensed us. I know he did."

"Then why didn't he turn us over to Stanton?" Serena asked.

"Maybe he's saving us for his own amusement," Vanessa said glumly.

"If we wait here, the monk might find us," Serena said. "He's helped us before."

A monk had suddenly appeared late one night and tried to comfort them. He had visited frequently after that, but still Vanessa hadn't trusted him. He never let them see his face, and if he was able to enter their room without using the door, then, Vanessa reasoned, he must have entered through a secret passageway. So why hadn't he let them use it to escape?

"But what if the Follower returns before the monk finds us?" Vanessa asked, not understanding Serena's hesitation. "It's risky to stay here."

"I'm too scared," Serena confessed.

Vanessa walked back to her and gently took her hand.

Serena was shivering. "I'm pathetic," she laughed. "You'd think I'd get used to feeling afraid by now."

"It's not something you can get used to," Vanessa said. "Not here, anyway."

"Let's get this over with." Serena took a deep breath and started down the stairs.

When they reached the cellar floor, Vanessa was overcome with a feeling that someone—or something—was watching them. She could hear strange gibbering from the corners, but nothing tried to attack them.

Fear sharpened her senses and, in spite of the darkness, she saw another door, high above them.

"There's probably a set of stairs that lead up to it," Vanessa whispered. "What do you want to do?"

"More than anything, I want to go home," Serena answered.

"Me, too," Vanessa said with growing resolve. "Is it worth the risk?"

"Yes," Serena said, tightening her hold on Vanessa's hand.

Together they found the stairs and stole up to the door. Then, cautiously, they opened it and stepped outside.

Flames sputtered inside lanterns that lined

the street and made shadows twitch across the towering houses. The stone faces of gargoyles glared down at them, but no Followers or Regulators lingered nearby. The street was empty except for a few pieces of trash and a discarded apple core.

"I can feel them watching us." Vanessa gazed up at the windows. "It's like everyone has been told to stay inside and let us escape."

"Then let's do it." Serena broke into a run. "Hurry."

Vanessa sprinted after her, eager to reach the portal that Catty had taken them to long ago. Maybe they did have a chance.

"Look!" Serena screamed after they had jogged for a few blocks. "There's the street." She dashed around the corner. "We made it." She spun around, letting her arms fly out, and laughed with true joy. "Now all we have to do is wait for the portal to open." She moved into the shadows beneath an overhanging balcony. "What's the first thing you're going to do when we get home?"

"Eat a hamburger with lots of pickles."

Vanessa felt intoxicated with happiness; she was really going home.

Serena leaned back and closed her eyes. "I can't wait to play my cello." She held her hands in position and pretended to rush the bow back and forth across the strings. She laughed, and the tone was cheerful, the way Vanessa remembered it.

"We'll go surfing," Serena said, "and see all the kids at school. I wonder what my father and Collin have been doing without me."

"I'm going to buy a huge bag of potato chips," Vanessa said, "and drive my car down to the beach."

"We'll eat ice cream until our heads ache from the cold," Serena said, giggling.

"And dance at Planet Bang," Vanessa added as she squeezed in next to Serena. "I can't wait to sing with Michael's band."

A hand grabbed Vanessa's arm and pulled her from their hiding place.

CHAPTER TWO

THE MONK STEPPED into the light and stood beside Vanessa, his face hidden in the hood of his robe. "I warned you not to escape," he scolded. His raspy voice made him sound ill. "How many times have I told you not to try?"

"The door was left unlocked," Serena snapped back, surprising Vanessa with her anger. "What did you expect us to do?"

"Catty's father, Adamantis, ordered the Regulator to leave the door open," the monk replied calmly. "He told everyone to remain inside and let you escape. His brutality is legend. No one will cross him."

"Why would he want us to escape?" Vanessa asked, still wary of the monk. "That doesn't make sense."

"He won't let you," the monk answered. "He plans to use your attempted escape to prove to the Atrox that you're still a threat and need to be destroyed."

"Maybe the portal will open before he can catch us," Serena said stubbornly. "I'm not going back. I can't. I'd rather die trying to escape than return to the way we were living."

"Don't be foolish." The monk gripped Serena's arm and forced her up. In the tussle, his hood slid back. He immediately dropped his hold and adjusted the cowl.

Serena stood beside Vanessa. "We're going to wait for the portal to open, aren't we?"

Vanessa was grateful for the fire that had returned to Serena's eyes, but she was noticing another change. The small hairs on her arms stood on end as static electricity filled the air.

"I think we'd better go with the monk," Vanessa said with growing nervousness. Blue sparks fluttered around them.

"Regulators," Serena said. Her shoulders slumped and she didn't move. "We were so close to going home."

Three cruel faces began to form within a swirling mix of shadow and flesh.

Vanessa pulled on Serena's arm. "Come on. Maybe we can find another portal."

Serena remained still, watching the monk.

"Are you willing to follow me now?" the monk asked, but he didn't wait for an answer. He ran off, his sandals slapping against the cobblestones.

Vanessa sprinted after him, her arms pumping hard.

Serena, cursing, could barely keep up. "I hate everything about this freaking place."

Twenty minutes later, they were still running. Vanessa's thighs burned, her feet ached, and her head pounded above her right eye.

"I can't go on," Serena said, holding her side.

She started trailing behind. Vanessa slowed down and stayed beside her.

A short distance later, the monk led them through a gateway into a field that surrounded an abandoned castle and stopped.

"Hide here while I find a portal that isn't guarded," he said. "Followers won't come to the castle, because they think it's haunted."

"Is it?" Vanessa looked up at the watchtowers. When she glanced back, the monk had already left.

"Hide in here?" Serena said pessimistically. "Could he have found a worse place?"

Vanessa nodded and started toward the footbridge that spanned the moat, her feet tromping over weeds. Nettles stung her legs, and burrs caught in her dress. "Maybe it won't be so bad inside."

"I doubt that." Serena walked beside her, still trying to catch her breath. "If the place can scare Followers, it must be really horrible."

As they crossed the drawbridge, the evening breeze filled with an electrical charge.

Serena gasped and turned around.

Vanessa brushed at the fuzzy feeling on her arms and looked out at the night. The massive rampart began to tremble. The vibration rushed through the ground and up her legs.

"Regulators," Serena said in a high, thin voice. "There must be an army of them materializing around us."

"The monk betrayed us," Vanessa said, looking for a place to hide.

"There." Serena pushed her forward just in time.

They ducked behind a rambling shrub and peeked out through its prickly vines.

"How many do you think there are?" Serena asked.

Vanessa shook her head. She didn't want to say the number that came to mind.

The air cracked and split. Shadows spilled from the fissures and formed into Regulators. Their eyes flashed with excitement, eager for the hunt. Their shrieking echoed off the castle walls.

"Something's really weird," Vanessa said.

"They're fighting each other like a pack of starved wolves. I've never seen that before."

"I don't think they were told to bring us back alive this time," Serena said. "They're acting like they were given permission to destroy us and each one wants the first bite of goddess."

Vanessa stared up at the castle's main tower. "We'll go up in the keep," Vanessa whispered. "Maybe we'll be safe there."

When they turned to leave, a velvet shadow formed from the air and blocked their way.

CHAPTER THREE

STANTON MATERIALIZED, his black cape swelling outward before settling again. He walked toward them with slow, easy steps, a lazy smile on his face. He brushed a hand through his shaggy blond hair.

Vanessa tried not to stare, but his piercing blue eyes were mesmerizing. She could feel his evil aura and sense his power.

"He's more handsome than ever," Serena sighed. "I hate him. Why didn't he come to see me?"

Vanessa didn't need to look at Serena to

know she'd never stopped loving Stanton, but did that mean she would willingly become a goddess of the dark to win him back? Serena didn't see light and dark as opposites but as two joined, necessary forces; the strength of both Hekate and Selene were inside her.

A flicker of remorse filled Stanton's eyes. He gazed affectionately at Serena, and then the tenderness disappeared, replaced by a frown. But the flash of emotion had been enough to tell Vanessa that he still loved Serena. That gave her an idea.

"Help us escape," Vanessa whispered urgently. "You were our friend once."

"Once," he replied. "No more."

His cruel expression sent a chill through Vanessa. Maybe she had misread the look he gave Serena.

"I can't believe I fell for you." Serena glared at Stanton.

He traced his finger down her neck. She didn't back away.

"Do you think I've come here to cause you more pain?" he asked.

"I don't know," Serena replied.

"I'm saving that for others," he said. "It's such a pity that you've chosen this for your end, when you could reign over darkness."

"Are you saying that I was a fool to love you?" Serena countered. Her eyes widened, and her pupils dilated. She stood motionless, in a trance, her body tense. She was trying to use her power and read his mind. That was her gift.

"Your power won't work in Nefandus," he said. "You can't read my thoughts, but I know what you're thinking and feeling. It's a mistake to still love me, Serena."

"Look deeper," she snapped back. "My real passion has always been my music."

"Yes, of course." A sensual smile formed on his lips. "But your gift only lasts until you're seventeen, and then you'll be mine, whether you love me or not."

"Why would you want me if you don't love me?" Serena challenged.

"Because you're the key," he said. "The one who can alter the balance between light and dark forces. Why else would I have ever wanted you?"

His answer startled Serena. She looked at Vanessa, her eyes wounded and glassy with tears.

Vanessa pulled her close. "We'll find another way to escape."

Stanton laughed at her bravery. "You were always so determined and recklessly bold. Can't you see that you've lost?"

"It's not over yet," Vanessa shot back. She had nothing to fear from Stanton. He had trapped her in one of his memories once, but while there she had tried to save a younger Stanton from the Atrox. As a result of that act of kindness, he could never harm her.

"I can't hurt you myself," Stanton said, seeming angered by her defiance, "but that doesn't mean I have to protect you from others."

Slowly, Vanessa turned and looked behind her.

Regulators crowded forward. Their eager whispers made her apprehension grow. Her chest tightened with new fear.

A brawny Regulator with a gnarled back

lumbered forward. His thick legs trod heavily on the ground. "Adamantis wants us to take the goddesses back to him."

"Adamantis ordered you to destroy them," Stanton said, correcting him. His eyes flashed, and the Regulator crouched nervously.

"Yes, *regis filius*." The Regulator groveled and went back to join the others.

"I'm returning the goddesses to the Atrox," Stanton said.

At once, the horde of Regulators began disappearing. Their wails of disappointment sounded like a sharp wind.

Stanton fell back, and, before his body hit the ground, he faded into ebony vapor. Night closed around Vanessa; at once she realized that Stanton was embracing her with his phantom arms. His energy hummed through her, forcing her to dissolve and become a shadow.

As soon as Vanessa and Serena were no more than black smoke, Stanton whisked them away, up and around the turrets and pinnacles, before heading out across the fields.

The ride was short. When Stanton released her, Vanessa materialized as she fell. She landed with a jolt and slid across a polished floor. Serena fell beside her. They lay sprawled together, all arms and clumsy legs, staring into each other's eyes, winded and frightened.

They became aware of people talking around them and helped each other stand up. Members of the Cincti, the Inner Circle, surrounded them. These men and women, dressed in long black robes, were the most powerful Followers and were favored by the Atrox. Vanessa could feel the evil coming off them. She bravely studied their faces, not flinching from the hatred in their eyes.

Then she saw her friend.

"Catty!" Vanessa squealed. She ran to her, her arms flying open. Serena raced behind her, screaming Catty's name.

"I thought you were dead." Vanessa stopped, horrified, and stepped back, bumping into Serena.

"What is it?" Serena asked. And, then she saw it, too. "I can't believe it."

The Phoenix crest adorned Catty's cape. Dread settled over Vanessa. Only the most powerful members of the Inner Circle were allowed to wear the emblem, and they had to commit an atrocity, something that pleased the Atrox, to win it.

"What have they done to you, Catty?" Vanessa asked. She knew her friend wasn't capable of anything evil.

"It doesn't matter," Serena said, with rising determination in her voice. "We'll find a way to free you from whatever spell they've cast over you."

The members of the Cincti laughed at her declaration.

"Why would I want to be freed?" Catty asked. "I earned this honor. Only the fiercest members of the Inner Circle are allowed to wear the Phoenix. It means I'm more enduring than an Immortal now. If something happens to my body, my spirit will live on. Cool, huh?"

"I know they did something to you, Catty," Vanessa said, blinking back her tears. "You could never—"

"Call me Atertra," Catty interrupted. "That was the name given to me at birth."

"I can't believe you'd do this freely." Vanessa studied her once best friend. Catty no longer wore a nose ring, earrings, or makeup. Her hair curled down her back, silken as before. Her face looked more beautiful, but she had lost her smile. Maybe she really had become a Follower.

"This is my heritage," Catty said frostily, seeming to read Vanessa's thoughts. "What do you expect from the child of a fallen goddess and a member of the Inner Circle?"

Vanessa clenched her jaw, sickened, unable to believe the intensity of her hatred for the one person she had thought would be her forever friend.

A man with thinning hair glowered at Vanessa. He placed his arm protectively around Catty. "Is there a problem, Catty?"

Vanessa recognized the voice at once. He was the man she had heard speaking to Stanton on the other side of the door when she and Serena were hiding in the cellar.

"This is my father," Catty said proudly. "Adamantis."

Adamantis smiled triumphantly and closed his eyes. Vanessa could feel him easing into her mind, searching for her fear. His eyes burst open when he found it. The pleasure in his gaze made her ill. His evil pulsed through her, and she couldn't break away from him.

"Such sweet terror," he murmured.

Serena grabbed Vanessa's arm and yanked her back, breaking the spell that Adamantis had cast over her. "Don't listen to him," she mumbled.

"The *frigidus ignis* awaits you," Adamantis said callously.

Vanessa and Serena turned bit by bit, afraid of what they would see.

"The cold fire," Serena whispered, pinching Vanessa's arm.

The *frigidus ignis* ceremony was the way the Atrox gave immortality to Followers who had pleased it. The cold flames burned away mortality and granted eternal life. Because Serena and Vanessa were Daughters of the Moon, they would also become fallen goddesses, Followers, against their will.

"What chance do we have?" Vanessa said, gazing into the fire, fascinated by the mix of frost and flames. The bitter cold made her shiver. Embers whirled around her, inviting her to step forward. She wanted to end her misery. Maybe this was the way.

When she stepped closer, the fire crackled and roared its welcome. She suddenly longed to embrace the blaze and let the ice form crystalline patterns all over her body.

Serena grasped Vanessa's wrist. "Don't you remember what Maggie told us?"

"If we step into the fire, we'll become fallen goddesses," Vanessa said dreamily. "I'm tired, Serena. I don't want to fight."

"You have to be invited by the Atrox," Serena warned, rousing Vanessa from her trance. "If you enter the fire without being invited, you'll suffer a horrible death. You need to be a *Lecta*, like me— a chosen one. The Atrox hasn't chosen you."

Vanessa turned back and stared at Catty's

father. He smiled thinly, and she knew with certainty that this was his plan. "Why does Adamantis hate me so much that he doesn't even want me to become a fallen goddess?"

"I don't know," Serena answered. "But he definitely wants you dead."

WITHOUT WARNING, a shadow slammed into Vanessa and knocked her away from the fire. She staggered, collapsing against Serena. The shape-shifter coiled around them both. Energy shot through Vanessa and, with a jolt, her body burst into a million specks that smashed back together, forming a murky silhouette of her arms and legs. Serena wavered next to her, whimpering, a shady outline of herself.

Regulators howled in fury and started to transform.

The shape-shifter, holding Serena and

Vanessa, soared over the members of the Inner Circle and bolted out the window, carrying the Daughters up into the cool night.

Regulators streaked after them with deadly speed. But the shape-shifter who had captured Vanessa and Serena flew faster and left the Regulators far behind.

In a few minutes, they descended into a forest. Pine needles tickled through Vanessa, and the lush woodland scent became part of her. Then her shadow thickened, and she materialized, the taste of evergreen still on her tongue.

"You?" Serena yelled, brushing her hair away from her face. "You're a shape-shifter. You're one of them, and you made me trust you."

"I saved your lives." The monk stood over Serena and Vanessa. As always, his face was hidden under the cowl.

"You should have told us you were a Follower," Serena said. "What are you planning to do with us now?"

He ignored Serena's outrage and started up a path that led through the trees.

"Hurry," he ordered in his raspy voice. "The door between Nefandus and Earth opens only when the demon star blinks."

The demon star was the eye of Medusa in the constellation of Perseus. The star was actually two stars that revolved around each other in an eclipsing binary. It gave the impression to the ancient Greeks that the eye of Medusa was blinking.

Serena looked at Vanessa. Her suspicion suddenly dropped away, replaced with excitement. "He found another portal. He didn't lie to us after all."

"The star has already dimmed in the earth's sky!" the monk shouted. "You have only minutes left."

Vanessa ran after Serena. At night, Nefandus had an artificial, gauzy sky that hid the moon because the residents hated its luminescence. In its place, red stars cast an eerie crimson glow over the trees.

"Here." The monk stopped in a clearing a few yards in front of them. The wind whipped his robe, thrashing the coarse material about, but he clutched his hood and held it down over his face. "The portal is open. You need to jump."

Vanessa stepped forward. Waves crashed over jagged rocks hundreds of feet below them. "How do you know there's a portal down there?" she asked.

When the monk didn't answer, she looked back. He wasn't there.

"He's already deserted us," Serena said angrily. "I don't know if we can trust him or not."

"That's a long way down," Vanessa said, studying the pointed rocks. "There's no way we would survive the fall."

"I'm not sure I have the guts to jump," Serena said. "It makes me dizzy just looking down."

Vanessa took Serena's hand. Her palm felt clammy. "We'll jump together."

"Let's do it," Serena said, squeezing Vanessa's fingers.

Vanessa swallowed hard, trying to get up the courage, but her knees trembled so badly she wasn't sure she'd be able to move. "You've always been a really good friend, Serena."

"Vanessa!" Serena yelled. "Don't start with

the mushy stuff. If you don't think we're going to make it, then we shouldn't jump."

"I'll shut up," Vanessa agreed but she rattled on nervously, "Do you remember when you snuck into my bedroom that first time? I thought you were so weird. You scared me to—"

"Don't reminisce," Serena ordered. "That's what people do before they die."

"Okay." Vanessa nodded. "This is it. On the count of three."

"I'm going to scream," Serena warned.

"Like you think I won't?" Vanessa asked. Her stomach fluttered with nerves, and her teeth were chattering.

"All right." Vanessa started to count. "One. Two."

Serena's hand was ripped away from Vanessa's.

"Run!" Serena screamed.

Vanessa spun around.

Regulators had snatched Serena. Her eyes were filled with panic as she rose up into the sky with them. Her body faded, then dissolved into the nightmare cloud of transforming Regulators.

"Serena!" Vanessa screamed, but her friend had disappeared already.

A pine cone snapped. Purple shadows clustered beneath the trees and grew thicker. Adamantis stepped forward, Catty by his side, a troop of Regulators materializing behind him.

"Get rid of her," Adamantis said in his haughty, nasal voice. "I can't bear the sight of her."

Three Regulators started forward, but Catty pushed them aside. "Vanessa is mine," she said. The Regulators stepped back, and Catty strode forward, bloodlust in her eyes.

"Don't," Vanessa pleaded. "Don't do this, Catty. We were best friends once. Don't you remember? You were always getting me into trouble and making me time-travel when I didn't want to. You wore those stupid bunny slippers and—"

"That was in another world," Catty interrupted. "In this one, depravity rules. Killing a goddess solidifies my power. And the fall off the cliff is definitely going to kill you." Catty rammed her hands against Vanessa's shoulders.

Vanessa fought for balance, but the ground gave way beneath her feet, and she fell. Air rushed around her, rumbling against her ears.

A strange grin covered Catty's face. She waved good-bye, then turned and stepped away.

Ocean spray misted over Vanessa. She was seconds from meeting death.

CHAPTER FIVE

FINE, STICKY THREADS spun around Vanessa and stopped her fall. She cried out as numbness swept through her. A soft, continuous *Om* filled the dark. She hated the passing, the time spent paralyzed between Earth and Nefandus. Catty had explained, on their first trip through, that everything on the earth was made from atoms, and that between those atoms were spaces in which other atoms spun, creating Nefandus. The two worlds existed side by side, intricately linked and superimposed upon each other.

Seconds ticked away as Vanessa's atoms reconfigured to fit into the environment on earth. When sensation returned, her lungs ached, her head throbbed, and her toes and fingers tingled. Immediately, the web holding her let go. She tumbled down and hit cold sand with a thump. She lay there, her arms spread out, and gratefully breathed in pure ocean air. She had missed the salty scent, the rumble of waves crashing to shore.

Her chest heaved; she could no longer hold back the tears. She cried for Catty and Serena, and then she cried for herself, because she knew she had to return to Nefandus and try to rescue Serena.

Slowly, the rhythm of the surf soothed her, and she stopped crying. A frothy wave rushed over her toes. High tide was setting in. She sat up and brushed off her arms, trying to get rid of the odd feel of Nefandus still clinging to her. With a start, she realized that the unpleasant, grimy feeling came from the air around her. Maybe she hadn't left Nefandus after all.

Cautiously, she stood up and looked down

the shoreline, then toward the strand and the city lights beyond. Without any doubt she was back in Los Angeles, near Venice Beach, but something was wrong. Palm trees swayed in the breeze, their glossy fronds tinged with pink. She stared out at the breakers pounding the shore. The phosphorescent waves had a reddish tint. She glanced up, searching for the source of light, and her heart lurched.

A full moon graced the heavens, but it looked eclipsed, rimmed in red, its luminescence almost gone. Maggie had warned her that if the Atrox ever won, the world, as she knew it, would change. But did that also mean the moon?

She smelled smoke beneath the briny tang of ocean air. Relief made her smile. Wildfires were burning somewhere, maybe in the Hollywood Hills or up in Malibu. A haze of ash and soot had shrouded the night and created the false impression that the moon was eclipsed. Smoke pollution could also explain the odd, sticky feeling on her skin.

Her stomach growled, and with the hunger

came a desperate need to go home. She wanted to see her mother, hear her comforting voice, and feel her hugs and kisses. Vanessa turned abruptly and started running. She leapt over the piles of the kelp that had washed ashore and then quickened her pace.

She had gone just a short distance when something thrummed against her chest. She stopped and glanced down, surprised to find her moon amulet glowing. Its magic hadn't died after all. Fiery pinks and blues glittered within the metal and cast an otherworldly light across the sand. Her amulet glowed only when Followers of the Atrox were near. She saw no one on the beach with her but she knew that she was no longer alone.

Most Followers in Los Angeles were Initiates: kids who had turned to the Atrox and wanted to prove themselves worthy of joining its congregation. She'd be able to see them sneaking up on her, and it would take more than a few to subdue her. But other Followers, shape-shifters, might pose a problem.

As if her thoughts had conjured one, a slice of darkness appeared in front of her.

"Goddess," Tymmie greeted her as he materialized. *Atrox* was tattooed on his shaven head. A wicked smile stretched over his face. "I saw you drop from the sky. What are you doing back in my world? I heard the Atrox was keeping you tight and cozy."

He belonged to a group of Followers who flaunted their badass behavior. They used the power of the Atrox, but also guns, knives, and fists.

"Get out of my way, Tymmie." She shoved past him.

He grabbed her around the waist and pulled her back against him. "You've spent a long time in Nefandus," he whispered against her cheek. "I thought you'd like bad boys by now."

Nefandus had hardened her. And she wasn't going to let him intimidate her as he once had. She turned slowly in his arms and gazed up into his eyes. "You're not bad enough, Tymmie."

She caught a glimpse of fear in his eyes, and

that pleased her. She turned and strode away from him, feeling powerful and like a goddess again, and wishing she were on solid ground so she could sway her hips and tease him.

"I just wanted to party with you," he shouted after her. "Goddess and bad boy—we could have had a freaking good time."

His laughter was joined by a raucous chorus of chuckles. She froze. How many Followers were with him?

"Vanessa." Her name came to her in a growing number of whispers. She summoned her courage and turned. Her stomach tightened. This time she did feel fear. Dozens of wraithlike shadows fluttered in the night air.

A black smudge molded itself into a tall figure with short spiked hair. "Hello, Vanessa," Karyl smirked. Her moon amulet cast a silvery glow across his face, but the light didn't seem to bother him as it once had. "Show us what you learned in Nefandus," Karyl taunted her. He slunk forward, and before she could dodge him, he gave her a wet smooch on the cheek. She wiped it away, then spun away from him and started to run.

Yvonne stopped her. She had grown her hair out and wore it straight. She looked like a Hollywood starlet in her slinky dress, but the black emptiness in her eyes made Vanessa wince. "Why are you back?" Yvonne asked suspiciously. She was an Immortal and had her own league of Followers in Venice Beach.

For the first time, Vanessa realized that they didn't know she had escaped. They obviously also hadn't heard that she was supposed to be dead, killed by her best friend Catty. Vanessa definitely didn't want word to get back to Catty and her father that she was still alive.

"Holiday," Vanessa answered flippantly; but her heart was racing with a surge of adrenaline.

She sensed them trying to read her mind and get the answers they needed. So, instead of dwelling on her worries as she walked away from them, she concentrated on her hunger. She pictured hamburgers, hot dogs, and French fries.

Another Follower formed in front of her,

guzzling a Coke. She felt like ripping the drink from his hands. And then she stopped, horrified. She could hear the Followers marching in the sand behind her, talking to one another and laughing. How many were there? She didn't really want to know.

She wished the other Daughters were with her, but, with a sinking feeling of despair, she realized she was alone—the last one—and vulnerable. Tianna was with Selene. Catty had turned to the Atrox. Serena was still imprisoned in Nefandus, or worse, dead. And Jimena had already turned seventeen and made her choice. That left only Vanessa. She needed to flee, but she couldn't run fast enough to escape so many pursuers. She hadn't been able to become invisible in Nefandus, but now she wondered if she still could. She concentrated on loosening her body.

Too late she realized that they had caught her plan in her thoughts. The Followers scrambled forward. Tymmie dived and tried to tackle her. Karyl flew into the air, transforming as he shot after her.

But her power was so eager to be free that, in an instant, she was gone. She floated, invisible, above them.

Tymmie slammed into the sand. "Where'd she go?" he asked, bewildered.

Vanessa sped toward the shops. The streets were crowded with sunburned people who had spent the day at the beach. She buzzed into a souvenir shop and hurried past the postcards and T-shirts in the entrance. Wind chimes jingled as she materialized near a magazine stand.

A newspaper headline caught her attention: SMOKE CREATES ILLUSION OF GHOSTS. She picked up the paper and read on. The article blamed thick smoke from the recent brush fires for the phantoms that people had reported seeing recently. All the sightings had taken place in a neighborhood near the Dungeon, a club in Hollywood where Followers hung out. Vanessa assumed that the Followers were becoming overly confident and bold and no longer felt the need to keep their existences a secret. They were probably transforming where people could see them.

She glanced at a sidebar, written by a psychologist who had a radio talk show. The title, "What to Do if Your Child Has Suddenly Become Afraid of the Dark," sent a chill through Vanessa as she imagined children awakening to find shape-shifters in their room. The psychologist suggested night lights, of course, and using fans to keep the smoke from settling. Vanessa shook her head without bothering to read more.

As she started to put the paper back, she glanced at the date. The newspaper slipped from her hand. She plopped herself down on a stack of magazines, dizzy and temporarily unable to think. She pressed her fingers into her forehead, trying to collect her thoughts.

Her seventeenth birthday was just two days away. Her goddess powers only lasted until she turned seventeen, and then there was a metamorphosis. It happened to all the Daughters. In two days she had to make the most important decision of her life: she could choose to lose her powers and the memory of her time spent as a goddess, or she could disappear. No one knew what happened to the girls who made the change and disappeared. Maggie had speculated that they became something else, guardian spirits, perhaps.

But Vanessa had a bigger worry: what would happen if her birthday came before she was able to return to Nefandus and free Serena? That worry unlocked a bigger one that had been in the back of her mind. She had seen the dreamy look on Serena's face when Stanton had suddenly appeared. Serena obviously still loved him. The other Daughters only had two choices, but Serena had always had a third. She could become a goddess of the dark. Serena had once confided in Vanessa that she felt a spiritual connection to Hekate and wanted to be initiated into the secret rites of the goddess. So, even if Vanessa did go back into Nefandus, would Serena want to be rescued?

Vanessa hurried outside and walked quickly down the street, already forming a plan. She'd turn invisible, catch the wind, and go to Jimena's apartment. Maybe Jimena had all her memories back now and would know what to do. That gave her hope.

Vanessa turned the corner, away from the crowd, searching for a private place where she could become invisible without anyone seeing her. The scrumptious smell of hamburgers sizzling on a street vendor's grill caught her by surprise. She stopped and breathed in the aroma. Overcome by hunger, she stole a pickle from the condiment bin, dipped it in the mustard, then slipped it into her mouth and crunched down. Flavors burst over her tongue.

Immediately, she realized her mistake. Tymmie had found her. She never should have paused.

"Didn't they feed you in Nefandus?" Tymmie dug into his pocket and pulled out a roll of bills. "I'll buy you a meal."

She turned to leave and bumped into Yvonne and Karyl.

"No where to run to," Yvonne said smugly. "Who would have thought that a pickle could have brought down a goddess?"

A congregation of Followers laughed. More inky shadows twisted closer, forming a barricade behind Yvonne.

"We've won," Karyl said with glee. "Admit it, Vanessa. We've almost blotted out the moon."

Power gathered in Vanessa's chest and spread to the tips of her fingers. She was going to disappear in a burst and leave them, but an odd sense of claustrophobia made her glance up. Shadows hovered above her, closing in around her. Even if she did turn invisible, she'd never be able to float through so many.

"Escape is impossible now," Tymmie whispered, his lips moving against her ear. He held the hamburger in front of her mouth. "Take a bite. Join the victors, and save yourself."

Vanessa shook her head. She was the last Daughter, the world's only hope, and she was caught. She glanced up through the shadows at the dying moon. Maybe this was the final eclipse.

CHAPTER SIX

AN '81 OLDSMOBILE sped down the street. Music pounded from inside, a heavy techno beat that vibrated through Vanessa and made the Followers turn. The car swerved, and its wheels jounced over the curb and onto the sidewalk. The bumper plowed through the inky shadows. Hellish screams filled the night as the shape-shifters scattered, only to return and hover in a menacing cloud.

Tymmie dropped the hamburger and held on to Vanessa. She wrenched herself free from his grip and ran toward the car. Spectral hands tried to catch her by the feet, but she hurtled over them.

The passenger-side door flew open.

"Get in!" Jimena yelled.

Vanessa threw herself onto the front seat and shut the door before the shape-shifters could sweep inside.

Jimena gunned the engine, then took her foot off the brake. The car blasted through the Followers with a screech of tires. Shadows smeared over the windshield, then whipped away, screeching furiously.

The car slewed from side to side and clipped a parked Jeep before it careened around the corner.

Jimena stared into the rearview mirror. "They're messing with the wrong homegirl when they mess with me," she laughed, thrilled with their escape.

Everyone had heard rumors about Jimena's gang adventures, and she had the scars to prove the stories were true. Two teardrops were tattooed under her eye: one for each stay in Youth Authority Camp. A small triangle of three dots was tattooed on the web between her index finger and thumb, a mark for *La Vida Loca*.

But right now Vanessa wasn't impressed with Jimena's bold rescue. "You hit them with the car," she said. "Maggie told us that we should never use the tools of the Atrox. Violence only feeds Followers and makes them stronger. They become invincible when we choose evil as our defense."

"That's old school," Jimena said, unmoved by Vanessa's comments.

"We're supposed to use the power inside us." Vanessa tried to buckle the seat belt, but her hands were shaking so badly she couldn't snap the lock. She gave up.

"Those rules don't apply to me," Jimena reminded her. "I'm not a Daughter."

"You were once," Vanessa replied angrily.

On Jimena's seventeenth birthday, she had chosen to give up her goddess powers and become a regular teen. But when she lost her memories of being a Daughter, other recollections of past lives had started coming back to her. She was the reincarnation of the ancient goddess Pandia, the daughter of Selene and Zeus, and she had come back to earth to stop a catastrophe.

"Would we have won?" Jimena asked as the traffic light turned yellow. She jammed her foot on the accelerator. The car zoomed through the intersection. "Did the two of us have a chance against so many?"

"No," Vanessa admitted reluctantly. "We were outnumbered." After a long sigh, she added, "Thanks." Then another thought came to her. "How did you know I had returned?"

"I used to have premonitions," Jimena said, "but, now, I guess you'd call me clairvoyant. I just know things. I don't remember what it was like to have the premonitions, because I was a Daughter then, and all those memories are erased, but this knowing what's going to happen in the future really freaks me out."

"What's the difference?" Vanessa asked. "It sounds the same to me."

"You told me that when I had the premonitions I'd *see* something, but the way I interpreted what I saw wasn't always right. Now, a voice whispers across my mind and tells me important things," Jimena explained. "Like today, I was just standing in the kitchen, and, wham, this voice inside my head says, *Vanessa's coming through the portal. She'll need your help tonight.*"

Jimena looked distressed. Vanessa wondered if the voice had told her more than she was telling Vanessa now.

"I almost didn't make it in time to save you, so maybe my powers aren't as strong as they should be yet," Jimena said; she glanced at Vanessa, seeming to see her for the first time. "Are you all right?"

"As good as I can be," Vanessa whispered.

They drove in silence for twenty minutes. When they reached Beverly Hills, Jimena parked the car under a jacaranda tree. Purple blossoms rained over the hood as the engine ticked, cooling down.

"I'm glad you're back." Gentleness had returned to Jimena's voice. "I missed you."

She touched the Medusa stone hanging around her neck, where her moon amulet had once been. The face of Medusa was carved into the charm. The flowing hair was a nest of coiling snakes. The stone protected Jimena and had the power to paralyze an enemy.

Vanessa had the eeriest feeling that the snakes were turning and staring at her.

"What happened to Serena?" Jimena asked, her eyes sad. She and Serena had been best friends.

Vanessa shook her head. "She's still in Nefandus. The last time I saw her, Regulators were taking her away."

"And Catty?" Jimena asked. She didn't look very hopeful.

"She's a Follower now," Vanessa said. Her chin quivered and she caught a sob. Her grief surprised her.

Jimena wiped the tears from her cheeks. "Tell me everything that happened," she said softly.

Vanessa began with the failed attempt to free Tianna and finished with her escape from Nefandus, when Catty had tried to kill her.

"I want revenge," Jimena said bitterly.

"Does that mean you'll help me rescue Serena?" Vanessa asked and hurried on, "Maybe we can find someone who will take us back into Nefandus now. We don't have enough time to wait for the portal to open if we want to save her."

"We can't go back to Nefandus," Jimena said. "I want to, but we can't."

The words surprised Vanessa. "We have to at least try to rescue Serena," she argued. "Serena used to be your best friend."

"She still is. But I didn't come back to rescue her," Jimena said sorrowfully. "I came back to stop the final eclipse."

Vanessa leaned forward and looked through the windshield, up at the ailing moon. "It doesn't look like you've been very successful so far," she said with a sinking feeling.

"You're the reason for the coming darkness," Jimena said quietly.

CHAPTER SEVEN

VANESSA AND JIMENA sat in a booth inside Johnny Rockets diner. Vanessa looked at her chocolate shake but couldn't drink it. The whipped cream on top had started to melt. She watched Jimena stuff a French fry coated with chili and melted cheese into her mouth.

"How can you eat?" Vanessa asked angrily.

"You need to eat," Jimena said. "You're too thin."

Vanessa glared at Jimena. "After telling me that you came back to earth to stop me from becoming a fallen goddess, you expect me to be able to eat? You told me I'm the reason for the final eclipse." Jimena's words still sent a chill through Vanessa. "Do you really think I can eat after that?"

"Your stomach was growling so loudly I figured you needed a meal," Jimena answered, trying to tease Vanessa out of her disconsolate mood. When Vanessa didn't respond, Jimena shrugged and picked up her hamburger. "It's good. Try it." She took a huge bite.

"How can you be sure I'm the one?" Vanessa repeated the question she'd already asked a dozen times. "You've been wrong before. Why are you so certain this time?"

Jimena grabbed a napkin and wiped the mayonnaise from her lips.

"When Stanton trapped you in his memory," Jimena explained, "the Atrox was able to see you before you were even born. It was so impressed with your bravery that it asked the Fates to weave your destiny into its own. The threads they spun destined you to become a Follower before your seventeenth birthday."

"That won't happen. I won't let it," Vanessa countered. "We make our own futures."

Two guys sitting at the counter turned and stared at Vanessa. She shot them an angry look. They turned back and hunkered over their food.

Vanessa raked her fingers through her hair, trying to calm herself. Then she remembered something. The heavy weight that had settled on her suddenly lifted. "I know you're wrong!" she said excitedly. "Remember the moon demon Hector?" She didn't wait for a reply. "The Atrox sent him to destroy me. Why would the Atrox do that if I'm destined to become a Follower? No way. That's proof you're wrong."

Jimena nodded and smiled.

Relieved, Vanessa picked up her burger and took a greedy bite. She closed her eyes, savoring the mix of pickles, onions, and melted cheese. "We'll go back into Nefandus and rescue Serena," she said, chomping on her food, "and then we'll figure out a way to stop the Atrox and give the light back to the moon."

Jimena waited until Vanessa had finished her

burger. Then she spoke: "Hector told you that he had been sent to destroy you. That's what he truly believed, but that was never what the Atrox planned. The Atrox used Hector to awaken the spirit of Pandora inside you."

Vanessa looked down at her plate. "Hector was going to take me away with him, to be his bride, and he would have if I hadn't freed him from the Atrox," she said.

"The Atrox would have stopped him." Jimena slurped up the last of her Coke through a straw. "Didn't you think it was odd that the Atrox didn't destroy you when you were imprisoned in Nefandus?"

Vanessa slumped against the back of the booth. "Serena and I talked about it all the time. We couldn't figure out why the Atrox kept us imprisoned when it could have executed us."

"It was waiting for the change to take place within you," Jimena said, "but your goodness was stronger than it had anticipated."

"I felt the evil growing inside me," Vanessa admitted. "But how can I bring unending misery to the world? You know me. My powers are so weak. I was never as powerful as you or Catty or Serena."

Another cheerful fifties song blared from the speakers. The feel-good music irritated Vanessa. She couldn't bear to hear another voice sing about true love and happiness. She slid out of the booth and ran outside.

Bikers, punkers, Goths, and starlets crowded the sidewalk on Melrose Avenue. Vanessa crossed the street, then leaned against a wall, exhausted, and watched the people strolling past her. She could never harm any of them. Surely Jimena was wrong.

"Vanessa!" Jimena pushed her way between two heavy-metal guys and joined her.

"I'd never hurt anyone," Vanessa said, looking down. "I couldn't."

"I'll protect you," Jimena said. "I have a plan."

"You do?" Vanessa lifted her head.

"Your birthday is only two days away," Jimena continued. "If you can hide from the

Atrox until you make your choice, then maybe you can escape your fate."

"Hide?" Vanessa laughed. The plan was ridiculous. No one could hide from the Atrox. She stepped away from Jimena and studied her closely. She was serious.

"Then I'll call forth the next generation of Daughters, and they'll save the world," Jimena explained.

"You?" Vanessa spit out the word. "What makes you think you're the next mentor?"

"Maggie told me," Jimena answered. "She sent me a telepathic message."

"How will four new Daughters be able to change what is happening?" Vanessa asked. "Don't you remember all the mistakes we made fighting the Atrox and its Followers?"

"The new Daughters won't make mistakes," Jimena answered. "Not with me as their mentor."

"You'll never measure up to Maggie!" Vanessa shouted, and immediately regretted her words. Jimena looked hurt.

"As Pandia, I was Maggie's first guide," Jimena said defensively, and then her confidence faltered. "I'm doing the best I can do," she whispered. Her defenses were down and without her bravado she seemed younger, more vulnerable, and scared. "It's not easy. I'm still Jimena inside here," she said, patting her temple. "But I can feel myself slipping away and becoming this Pandia." Tears rimmed her eyes. "I don't want to lose myself."

For the first time Vanessa realized how frightening the change must be for Jimena. She felt suddenly sorry for her friend and wished she'd given her more support.

"I wish Maggie were here," Vanessa whispered, rubbing Jimena's back. "She'd know what to do."

"The Atrox killed her," Jimena said quietly, staring out at the street. "You must have figured that out by now. You know she never would have deserted us."

Vanessa closed her eyes. "How?"

"The Atrox took away her immortality,"

Jimena said slowly. "As she was dying, she contacted me."

"Her death must have been horrible," Vanessa whispered.

When Maggie was young, she had pleaded with the goddess Selene to let her live to see the Atrox destroyed. But before Selene could answer her plea, the Atrox gave Maggie immortality. Because she had failed to ask for perpetual youth, she had condemned herself to age forever. Selene had given her an elixir to counteract the aging, but her immortality had remained a gift that the Atrox could take back whenever it wanted.

"I have something that Maggie gave me." Vanessa tugged on the neckline of her dress, revealing the delicate floral pattern on her skin. "This tattoo appeared the night I performed a ritual with Maggie before I went off to fight the moon demon. She told me the tattoo had magical powers to protect me, but now I wonder if anything can."

"I'll protect you," Jimena said. "I promise."

"I know you will," Vanessa said, even though

she thought Jimena's plan was foolish. "I'll go into hiding, but I need to see my mother first. It might be . . ."

She couldn't bring herself to say the words, but the look on Jimena's face told her that she understood. Vanessa might never have the opportunity to see her mother again and tell her how much she loved her.

"I'll give you a ride." Jimena started toward her car.

Vanessa shook her head. "I don't think Followers are still chasing us. They're too busy celebrating their victory. I'll be safe." She shrugged, not wanting to tell Jimena her real reason. She wanted to be alone when she saw her home again for the first time after so long.

"My house is really close. I'll be fine." Vanessa hugged Jimena as if she would never let her go. If everything that Jimena had told her was true, then the next time Vanessa saw her, they might be enemies.

Jimena pulled back and gave her a saucy smile. "You're going to survive this," she said, trying to bolster Vanessa's confidence. *"Sin duda."*

"You'll be a great mentor," Vanessa said encouragingly as she blinked to keep her tears from showing. "The new Daughters will love you as much as we loved Maggie. Good——"

Jimena clasped Vanessa's arm tightly, surprising her. "Don't say good-bye," she said firmly.

Vanessa nodded and hurried away. She stepped into the nearest alley, and, when she was certain no one was watching, she lifted her hands to the fading moon. A pleasant ache rushed through her as she released herself. She loved the stretch of bone and muscle as her molecules loosened and broke free from gravity. At last, she leaned back and let the night catch her.

Invisible, she road a breeze up and over the rooftops, then hooked on to an easterly wind that was filled with ash and smoke from the fires. She floated with it toward her neighborhood. Impulsively, she somersaulted, then dived up and down. Joy raced through her. She had missed her gift—her ability to become invisible—and the thought surprised her, because more than anything, she had wanted to be like everyone else. She had regarded her ability as a curse for most of her life. It had always made her feel like an outsider, a freak who didn't fit in. She had lived in fear that someone would discover her secret and then kidnap her and put her on display in a sideshow in some circus. If it hadn't been for Catty, she probably wouldn't have had any real friends.

Thinking about Catty made her wonder again how Catty could have betrayed her. Even if she had become a loyal Follower, it was hard for Vanessa to imagine that their friendship had meant so little to Catty that she would have wanted to kill Vanessa rather than just turn her into a fallen goddess.

Vanessa tried not to think about the look on Catty's face when she pushed her off the cliff, but a vivid image came to the front of her mind anyway. The memory brought too many conflicting emotions with it.

Sudden, intense rage zipped through Vanessa and made her molecules crash back together. She materialized with a jolt, then braced herself, swinging her arms, and hit the ground running before tripping over someone's garden hose and sliding over wet grass.

A neighbor might have seen her reform and fall from the air, but she no longer cared who knew her secret. She was less than a block away from home. She picked herself up and galloped down the sidewalk.

"Mom!" she screamed. "I'm home!"

CHAPTER EIGHT

VANESSA RAN UP the walk to the small Craftsman-style house that had always been her home. Her red '65 Ford Mustang was parked in the drive under the carport. She patted the bumper, then swiped her fingers over the hood as she hurried past it. Memories of rides with her friends flashed through her mind.

She rushed around the overgrown shrubs to the backyard and imagined her mother jumping up from her worktable and running across the kitchen to embrace her.

Out of breath, she yanked at the door. It was

locked. That surprised her. She quickly lifted the mat, pulled out the key, and unlocked the door.

As she stepped inside, familiar scents washed over her. She shut the door and breathed in the lingering bouquet of her mother's perfume, the faint aroma of oregano, and the lemony smell of furniture polish.

"Mom," Vanessa said, choking on her sobs.

Silence answered her.

She stepped into the kitchen and flicked on the light. Photographs of her own face startled her. Pictures of Vanessa were stuck to the refrigerator, the cupboard doors, and the wall. The array of snapshots momentarily stunned her. She had missed her mother but, until that moment, she hadn't realized how much her disappearance had crushed her mother's world.

Three different flyers were pinned to the wall above the calendar, each one with Vanessa's photograph and her mother's typed-out plea for Vanessa to come home. She wished she had told her mother the truth long before and saved her some of this anguish. Her mother would still have grieved, but at least she wouldn't have blamed herself for Vanessa's disappearance.

She eased over to her mother's worktable. A large bulletin board hung on the wall above the clutter. Her mother had called it her inspiration board. On the night that Vanessa had been kidnapped, a bunch of sketches and bold-colored swatches had covered it. Now, newspaper clippings and magazine articles were tacked over the drawings and pieces of material.

Vanessa sat down in her mother's chair and took down the closest clipping. She skimmed over it and huffed in disbelief.

According to the article, the aurora borealis had caused the power surges and outages on the night that Vanessa and her friends had been kidnapped. The northern lights were also blamed for the breakdown in telephone communication for both cell phones and land lines.

The article went on to say that although sightings of the northern lights over Los Angeles were rare, the aurora borealis had been seen as far south as Mexico City. Scientists at Caltech stated that when electrons collided with the nitrogen in the atmosphere, a blue tinge was seen in the northern lights. The black lightning, that Angelenos had reported seeing, was actually no more than shifting bands of deep blue color in the aurora borealis. The ribbonlike arcs had been triggered by fierce solar activity.

Vanessa set the clipping aside, amazed that scientists had been able to explain away all the supernatural strangeness of that night.

The phone rang. The loud sound made her jump. Her mother's voice came over the outdated answering machine: *"I'm in Buffalo. Please leave a message. Vanessa, if this is you, sweetie, come home. I'll be back in time for your birthday."*

A beep followed. A male voice left a message about the car needing its tires rotated.

More sadness settled over Vanessa. She doubted that she would survive until her birthday, but she didn't want her mother to go on believing that she had run away from home. She picked up a piece of paper and a pen and began to write.

Dear Mom,

I know you think I ran away from home but that's not true. I love you and the life we had together, but there are things about me that I never had the courage to tell you. I kept them secret because I was afraid you wouldn't love me if you knew the truth. I can become invisible. Don't laugh. It's true.

Do you remember the night when I was a little girl and I had that really bad nightmare? Even though you could hear me crying, you couldn't find me anywhere. That was the first time I became invisible. I woke up and couldn't see my body. I was terrified. You ran into my room to comfort me but when I lifted my arms for you to pick me up, you couldn't see me, either. That scared me even more.

When I finally materialized, I looked hideous. Everything was put together wrong. I didn't know how to use my power then. I still don't. But when I woke up the next morning, thankfully, I looked normal again. I was too scared to tell you what had happened, because I thought I'd done something *wrong. And I was worried that you wouldn't love me if you knew the truth. How could you love someone who was so different?*

A while back I asked you if you believed there was a goddess of the moon. That was the night I discovered that I am a goddess, a Daughter of the Moon. I know that sounds crazy but it's the truth. I'm here to keep hope alive and to defend people against an ancient evil called the Atrox. It kidnapped me the night I disappeared, and captured Serena and Catty, too.

When my friend Tianna persuaded the Atrox to release us, instead of fleeing I convinced them to stay and rescue Tianna. I didn't know then that Tianna wasn't a real person. She was something the Atrox had created, so we never would have been able to free her.

Vanessa stopped writing.

After a moment's pause, she crumpled the paper. Her mother would never believe a word that Vanessa had written. The letter would convince her mother only that she had lost it—that she'd become a druggie who lived on the streets. Maybe it was better to let her mother go on thinking that Vanessa had run away.

She threw the wadded paper into the trash can under the table. Then she walked upstairs to her bedroom and stood in the doorway, feeling unable to go inside.

She had once loved to lie on her bed in the dark and gaze out her open window at the moon. But now she knew she would never feel secure in her room again. She had been in bed, reading a book and enjoying what she had thought was a thunderstorm, when her shutters had smashed open and the Atrox had kidnapped her.

The same fear washed over her even now as she realized that she was never going to feel safe until the Atrox was destroyed. But how could she fight it alone? Her mood was quickly sinking past sadness into despair.

She stepped across the hallway and entered her mother's storage room. She remembered being there with her friends and dressing up in the clothes that her mother had designed for the movies.

Her mother was always a year or two ahead of the current styles. That was part of her job. But not everything she designed became a trend. Vanessa picked up a pair of baggy shorts with thick suspenders. She smiled, wondering if her mother wore them with the polka-dotted sneakers on the floor. The shorts would most likely become one of her failures.

The outfits that her mother wore had sometimes embarrassed Vanessa, but just then she'd have been happy to suffer one of those humiliating moments if it meant she could see her again.

She pulled on a biker-chick jacket and stepped over to the full-length mirror to see how it looked.

She glanced at her reflection and froze. A woman stood behind her.

CHAPTER NINE

P

ALE MOONLIGHT emanated from the woman, a mysterious glow that enveloped Vanessa and calmed her. She knew intuitively that she was gazing into the face of the goddess Selene.

"The Atrox is winning," Selene whispered, "because everyone is giving up. Hasn't my moon taught anyone the lessons of life?"

"The phases of the moon teach us that our darkest moments lead us to our brightest," Vanessa recited, but her mood had grown so dark that she wanted to add: "yada yada yada." Too much had happened to her. She no longer believed in the strength of hope.

"I see." Selene smiled sadly and brushed a hand through Vanessa's hair. "We never know what the future will bring us."

"That's right," Vanessa said miserably. "Every time I think things can't possibly get any worse, they do."

"You miss your friend Catty," Selene said.

"She's one of them now, a Follower, and she didn't deserve this kind of end. She was always so fun-loving and . . ." Vanessa couldn't go on. The memory of who Catty had once been and what she was now was too painful to recall.

Selene turned away and began rummaging through the dresses hanging on the rack. She held up a slinky sundress. "This one. Definitely, this one. Put it on. You can't go to Planet Bang dressed as you are."

Vanessa gawked at her. "I can't go to Planet Bang at all," she protested. "Jimena wants me to—"

"Has anyone ever been able to hide from the Atrox?" Selene interrupted and cocked her head prettily. "Don't you want to see Michael?"

"More than anything," Vanessa confessed. He was the only friend she had left, unless something had happened to him, too. The way her luck was going, it probably had. A new worry began gnawing at her. And it wasn't like she didn't have enough on her mind already.

"Why do mortals make themselves suffer so?" Selene began searching for shoes to go with the dress. She pulled out a pair of strappy sandals. "During the dark moon times, when people feel so hopeless, I watch them cower and hide, but my moon always brings light again."

"Have you looked at your moon lately?" Vanessa asked.

"Whether you stay here moping—"

"I'm not moping! Jimena told me to hide," Vanessa said with rising anger. "And don't you think I have a right to be sad, with everything that's happened to me?"

Selene placidly continued, as if Vanessa had not spoken, "—or whether you go dancing, the future will still find you."

"So, you're telling me that the Atrox wins," Vanessa said.

"Did I say that?" The goddess looked at Vanessa quizzically. "Surely I didn't. That would mean I've given up, too."

"All right. So I feel like giving up—my life hasn't been easy lately." Vanessa tried hard not to cry, but tears slid down her cheeks and dropped onto the dress that Selene was holding out to her.

"With two days left you're going to surrender?" Selene asked. "Two days can change the world."

"Two days," Vanessa repeated sadly. "It's not enough time, and I have no one to help me."

"It's odd to me, Vanessa," Selene went on, "that you hide the incredible energy that you have inside you and you make yourself miserable, denying your power. I don't know what you gain, but I do know what you lose by denying who you really are."

Vanessa stared at her. "Aren't you going to help me?"

"I just did," Selene replied.

"You did?"

Selene smiled sweetly and caressed Vanessa's cheek. Her hand was warm and comforting. "Maybe you should have paid more attention to being a goddess. After all, that is what you are, Vanessa. You're definitely not the person you pretend to be."

"Are you trying to make me feel better?" Vanessa asked with sudden annoyance. "Because if you are, it's not working."

Selene started toward the door. "Don't let the next two days go by unlived," she warned. "Control your destiny. Even the bleakest moments can bring you joy if you look up at my moon and understand that suffering is sometimes required to grow you into the person you need to become."

"Your moon is dying!" Vanessa shouted.

Selene left the room, and Vanessa rushed after her. She had a million questions and wished she hadn't wasted time arguing. The hallway was empty except for a fading white glow.

Vanessa tromped back to the mirror and studied her reflection. Maybe Selene was right. If she only had two days left, why waste it? Jimena's plan was never going to work anyway.

An hour later, Vanessa walked up the street toward Planet Bang. The music grew louder and pulsed through her. Kids stood behind metal barricades, waiting to be frisked by the security guards so they could go inside. Already she could feel her mood lifting. She thought of Michael and a thrill swept through her. How long had it been since she'd seen him? She hoped he hadn't found someone else.

"Vanessa?" A hand touched her back. She turned, and Derek hugged her. He rocked her back and forth, squeezing hard. "I can't believe you're here." He pulled away from her. "You look more gorgeous than ever." Then he leaned in closer. "Is Tianna with you?"

"Tianna won't be coming back," Vanessa whispered.

"She told me she was getting anxious to leave

L.A." he said, "but I'd kinda hoped she'd come back, at least for a visit."

"Don't you remember what happened?" Vanessa asked.

"What?" He looked puzzled. Derek had known their secret, but apparently something had happened to make him forget.

"Vanessa!" Corrine screamed, her friends Jessica and Melanie trailing behind her as she ran to Vanessa. "I can't believe you're back."

All three looked super girlie in see-through halter tops with skinny straps and lacy push-up bras underneath. The gauzy material showed off their belly rings and flat stomachs.

"We all knew Tianna was a runner—" Corrine began, her hands fluttering deliberately, to make her gold bracelets jangle.

"She was a tramp." Jessica swayed and caught herself. Her platform sandals were too high.

"Tianna wasn't a tramp," Derek said tiredly, as if they had had this argument many times before. "You were just jealous of how beautiful she always looked."

"Like I'd ever want to look like her," Jessica snapped back, scowling.

Corrine rushed on, "Everyone was shocked that you went with her, Vanessa. That just wasn't like you at all. I tried to stop all the rumors, but—"

"What rumors?" Vanessa asked.

"You can't just run off and not expect people to talk," Jessica said.

"No one was surprised about Catty." Melanie adjusted her minitiara. "And Serena had a reputation for being the queen of weird, so her disappearance was definitely not a shock."

"There was nothing weird about Serena," Vanessa argued. "And Catty was—"

"Please," Corrine interrupted. "I know you have to defend them, because they were your friends, but they were never popular like you."

"How could they be?" Melanie smirked. "Do you remember the way Serena dressed?"

"I liked her style," Vanessa countered, feeling her sadness give way to anger. She gazed at them, stunned. She had always been nice to Corrine and her friends, but now she wondered why she had tried so hard to be liked by people who were obviously mean-spirited.

"Whatever," Corrine said dismissively.

"Still, no one could believe you'd run off and live on the streets," Derek said. "Especially not Michael."

"Is he here?" Vanessa asked. She didn't like the quick exchange of glances between Corrine and Derek.

"Since you ran away, he's become—" Derek looked at Corrine for help.

"Morose . . ." Corrine offered. "But that just makes him cuter. I've always liked dark, mysterious guys."

"He's, like, a poet." Jessica practically swooned. "He writes so many songs about love and loss."

"I love the brooding way he looks at me. It sends shivers up my spine." Melanie bit her lip. "I'd give anything to spend one night with him."

Vanessa didn't need to hear more. She had to find Michael. She hoped he hadn't become a Follower. She hurried away from them without saying good-bye.

Corrine ran after her, leaving the others behind. "You can't go without giving me all the details. What was it like living on the street with so many guys?"

Vanessa's mouth fell open. "Is that what you think?"

Corrine shrugged. "Other kids are saying worse, especially because Tianna had such a reputation."

"She didn't have a reputation until you started saying bad things about her," Vanessa said as they turned the corner and started down an empty street.

Corrine smirked. "I only repeated the things I'd heard."

"That's not true," Vanessa said.

"Please," Corrine said with a wave of her hand. "I know what Tianna was. I just don't like to say the word."

Vanessa had always feared that someone would discover her secret, but suddenly she no longer cared. She freed her molecules and vanished in front of Corrine.

Corrine screamed and looked completely terrified. The fear on her face satisfied Vanessa, but only for a second. Then her niceness kicked in, and she felt horrible for what she had done. She circled back. Maggie had told her that it was amazing how far people would go to deny what they saw when they encountered the supernatural. Vanessa hoped that was true.

"I worked as a magician's assistant in a circus." She whispered her lie into Corrine's ear. "This is just one of the tricks."

"Cool." Corrine's eyes brightened, and she stood taller. She smoothed down her hair, then strutted back around the corner to her friends. "Vanessa ran off with a circus. Can you imagine? She told me everything."

"Was she a clown?" Melanie joked.

"She worked as a magician's assistant," Corrine said.

Melanie and Jessica giggled.

Vanessa didn't wait to hear more. She buzzed away, eager to see Michael.

VANESSA RACED THROUGH the night, low to the ground, taking in the rich scents of grass and soil. Michael's Volkswagen bus was parked in the drive in front of his house. His dad had owned it in the sixties. The psychedelic pink and orange flowers painted on the side had faded, and the bumper was rusted and almost falling off, but seeing the van filled Vanessa with joy. Michael was home.

She skimmed over the brick walkway, then up the side of the house, and brushed through the honeysuckle that climbed the trellis to the second floor. The blossoms flittered through her and released their sweet smell.

With increasing excitement, she hovered near the first window and peered inside. When she didn't see Michael, she flew to the next one and looked through the glass.

Michael sat on his bed, bare-chested, playing his acoustic guitar, his gorgeous black hair hanging in his face. Tattoos of barbed wire circled his tanned arm. She had loved to trace her finger over the lines and feel the hard muscles beneath his warm skin.

She seeped through a crack and entered his room. Her motion stirred the air and made the curtains flutter, but Michael didn't seem to notice. He was too intent on playing his song.

A framed picture of the two of them sat on his dresser. She swooned; he hadn't found anyone else. Her school picture, the edges tattered and worn out, was propped up against the lamp on his nightstand. Did he kiss it each night before he went to sleep?

She swirled down and curled around him,

cradled in the heat radiating off his body. His clean, soapy scent enveloped her.

Each time he plucked a guitar string, the thrum resonated through her. He sang about lost love. She had forgotten the mesmerizing power of his voice. She wanted to materialize right there on his lap and kiss him. There was nothing Follower about him.

She glanced up and studied his handsome face, his sultry eyes. Emotions she hadn't felt while she was imprisoned in Nefandus prickled through her. She had forgotten all the delicious sensations that being close to him made her feel. She sighed, shocked, when her voice made a sound.

Michael's head jerked up.

Panic-stricken, Vanessa untangled herself from Michael and swept over his head. Her sudden movement ruffled his hair. He looked puzzled and touched his face.

She floated up to the ceiling. Spasms shuddered through her, and she dropped three inches. She was starting to re-form. With wild, frantic strokes, she tried to swim through the air to the bedroom door.

"Damn," she whispered.

She fell, completely solid. Her shoes clunked on the floor.

Michael jumped up, startled. He spun around and stared down at her. "Vanessa!"

It took her a moment to get rid of the dizzy confusion in her head, and then she stood up as gracefully as she could. "Hi, Michael."

"I didn't know you were back." He set his guitar down.

"I'm sorry to barge in on you like this." She cringed. Could she have possibly said anything stupider?

He didn't seem to notice. "Dang, it's good to see you," he said.

Her stomach muscles tensed. She was eager to see what would happen next. But he didn't run to her and swing her into his arms as she had always imagined he would. Maybe she had to be the first one to act. She had always thought she'd lose her virginity to Michael, and, now, standing before him with only two days—maybe not even that long—left before the Atrox claimed her, she knew what she wanted to do.

But when she stepped toward him, he winced and turned away from her. Surprised by his rejection, she glanced at her reflection in his dresser mirror. Nefandus had changed her, but she didn't think she looked that bad. Then, too, maybe Michael could see the fallen goddess in her eyes.

She turned and ran from his room.

CHAPTER ELEVEN

HEARTBROKEN, VANESSA bolted down the stairs, taking them two at a time in spite of her high-heeled sandals.

The TV blared in the living room. Michael's grandfather was lounging on the couch, a bowl of popcorn on his lap. He looked up, taken aback when he saw her.

"Vanessa!" he called, his face breaking into a smile. "I didn't know you had come home."

"Hi, Mr. Saratoga!" she yelled.

When she glanced at him, she lost her footing. She stumbled off the last step and collided with the front door, then banged against the wood and groaned.

Michael's grandfather hurried toward her. "Did you hurt yourself?"

"I'm fine," she answered.

Michael thundered down the stairs behind her. She was too flustered to face him. She opened the door, squeezed past his grandfather, and ran outside, across the lawn and into the shadows. When she was sure no one could see her, she threw herself into the air and burst into a million fragments.

"You didn't tell me that Vanessa had come back," Michael's grandfather said as he followed Michael down the front walk.

"I just found out." Michael looked up and down the street. "She must have snuck into the house."

His grandfather looked worried. "Is she all right? She's been gone for a long time."

"I don't know," Michael replied. "She looked different."

Vanessa swept back and hovered over

Michael. Her tears fell on his head. He glanced up. She wondered if he could make out her sad image in the flutter of specks beneath the trees.

The automatic sprinklers cycled on. Michael and his grandfather ran back to the porch, but neither went inside.

"I hope she's okay," his grandfather muttered, but Michael didn't respond.

Vanessa left them and sped through the night, anxious to reach Jimena's apartment. She was going to throw a tantrum, the biggest one ever. She planned to kick and scream and cry and eat a gallon of cherry vanilla ice cream. She didn't understand why Selene had visited her, and she wished now that she had never let the goddess talk her into going to Planet Bang. It had been a disaster, but that fit just perfectly into the catastrophe that had become her life.

As she headed toward La Brea Avenue, something other than wind whipped through her. She slowed, expecting to see a flurry of leaves, but there was nothing that could explain the strange feeling.

When she eased out from under the shelter of the trees, something raced through her again. She curled around, trying to see what it was. An unnatural shadow slammed down on her. A shape-shifter had found her.

Focusing her energy on speeding away, she twisted up, then down, but couldn't free herself. The shape-shifter was forcing her to materialize.

Her molecules smashed together. She was still eight feet off the ground. She swung her arms out and tried to land on her feet, but the shape-shifter had also formed. His body hit her back, throwing her forward. She tumbled into a hedge.

When she tried to stand and get away, her legs buckled. Her knees hit the ground, and she sprawled out with a moan.

The shape-shifter landed with a loud thud on the sidewalk behind her.

In spite of the pain, Vanessa made herself get up. She undid the straps on her sandals, kicked them off, and, then, limping, ran.

At the next corner she realized no one was chasing her. She glanced over her shoulder.

The monk lay on the ground.

She crept back to him.

"Are you all right?" she asked, surprised to see him.

When he didn't answer, she knelt beside him and gently pushed his hood back.

"Stanton," she whispered, stunned, and then she gently nudged his shoulder. He was an Immortal. He couldn't die, and yet he lay lifeless before her.

CHAPTER TWELVE

VANESSA'S MOON amulet glowed and lit Stanton's face. Unconscious, he looked angelic, but the evil coming off him was stronger than when he was conscious and in control. Even though she wanted to flee, she pressed her fingers on his wrist and felt his pulse. The beats were weak and far apart, loping oddly.

She didn't know what to do. She couldn't call an ambulance or take him to a hospital. The doctors would have been able to feel his aura; and what if he turned into a shadow in front of them? She wondered briefly how a scientist would account for that but she had no doubt that they would find a logical reason for his disappearance. So far, they had explained away every supernatural event that had taken place in Los Angeles.

Stanton blinked. When his eyes opened, he seemed unable to focus them. "I tried to rescue Serena," he whispered groggily. "I failed."

"Is she all right?" Vanessa asked.

"I don't know," Stanton mumbled. "The Atrox stopped me. It wounded me, but I got away. I had to, because I needed to find you. You're Serena's only hope now. You have to return to Nefandus and rescue her."

Vanessa wondered what had happened to Serena, but she was also cautious. Stanton's weakness could have been a ploy to hold her until Regulators arrived.

She glanced down the street, but didn't see anything to make her wary. She tried to convince herself that Stanton wasn't her enemy. After all, he had once tricked a Regulator into protecting her from the moon demon. And now more than ever she needed him as her ally, because if there was any chance to do so, she wanted to rescue Serena.

"What happened?" she asked at last.

"I heard rumors that Serena was going to be forced into the cold fire," Stanton said as he started to drift off. His eyelids were fluttering. "I was surprised the Atrox hadn't invited me to the ceremony, but then I feared Adamantis was behind it and doing something to her." Stanton became unconscious again.

Gently, Vanessa lifted his head and cradled it in her lap. His forehead felt clammy.

With a start, he awakened and tried to sit up.

"Why did you try to rescue her disguised as the monk?" Vanessa asked. "That was too dangerous."

"This isn't a disguise," he countered. "I am the monk."

"I know you're lying," Vanessa said. "You have an aura. The monk never had one."

"Do you think that's something I can't control?" he asked.

At once, the air around her felt normal again; his evil aura had vanished.

Stanton tried to smile at her surprise, but he grimaced instead and then groaned. "I couldn't tell you or Serena that I was the monk, because Regulators were reading your thoughts. They had already reported to the Atrox that the monk was visiting you."

"Why didn't you help us escape a long time ago?" Vanessa asked with bitter frustration. "When you found us at the castle, instead of taking us back to the Atrox, you should have let us go."

"You wouldn't have been able to get away from the Regulators," Stanton said weakly. "Adamantis had given them permission to destroy you. Their hunger was fierce."

A sound made Vanessa jump. She pressed her fingers on Stanton's lips, signaling him to be quiet, but he continued talking deliriously, his words running together: "I swear I would have helped you escape if it had ever been safe. I protected you when Adamantis found you hiding in the cellar. He wanted you to run so he could catch and kill the two of you himself. The hunt is everything to him."

Vanessa tried to shush him. She needed to concentrate because she had heard something other than the rustle of palm fronds. But Stanton chattered on. Was his constant jabbering a cover to hide the approach of Regulators? Maybe he had deceived her after all.

"When I found you and Serena in the abandoned castle, I took you back to the Atrox's palace because that plan felt safe to me," Stanton continued. "I didn't know that Adamantis had already started the cold fire ceremony. If I had, I never would have taken you back there. Adamantis knew that Serena would become a fallen goddess, but he also knew that you hadn't been chosen to enter the flames. He was excited to watch you suffer a horrible death."

Vanessa wanted to know the reason Adamantis was so intent on killing her, but just then she had a more immediate concern. The air had shifted, and she feared that someone was coming through. Most Regulators and many

Followers, like Stanton, had the power to go back and forth between Nefandus and Earth without waiting for a portal to open. Maybe Regulators had chased Stanton into this dimension.

Her heart sank. "You have to be quiet," she warned.

But Stanton ignored her. "Once the Atrox started the *frigidus ignis* for Serena, I couldn't stop the ceremony without questions arising about my loyalty," he said before blathering on about the politics and intrigue among the Followers. At last he came to his point: "In order to save Serena, I had to slip back into a corner and put on the monk's robe again, but this time it was a trap. The Atrox had used Serena to lure the monk into showing himself. I didn't know. How could I? The Atrox hadn't told me its real plan. That was the first time since I became Prince of Night that the Atrox hadn't confided in me. It trusts no one now." He convulsed and passed out again.

In the absence of his constant chatter, Vanessa became aware of a soft tremor. She studied the shadows beneath the trees until she had found what she feared would be there. Ripples shimmered like heat waves beneath the glossy leaves of a cottonwood tree, but she knew if she stepped over to that spot she would feel a dreadful cold, not warm air. Something was traveling from Nefandus into the earth realm.

She had to get Stanton to safety. Once he recovered, if he ever did, then together they might still be able to save Serena. In the past she had been able to make others become invisible with her, but her anxiety was too high, and she doubted she could do it. Instead, she stood up and tugged on his arm, trying to pull him into the darkness near a house.

His eyes opened and he stared up at her, seeming not to comprehend what she was doing, or even to sense her urgency. Maybe he had hit his head on the concrete. He could have a concussion, she supposed. That would explain why he seemed so punchy and dazed.

A soft hiss filled the night, and she cursed silently. Someone had definitely come through and was hiding now.

"What is it?" Stanton asked.

"I think Regulators followed you from Nefandus," she whispered.

"Then leave me, and get away," he said in a low voice. "Go. You're Serena's only hope. Tell me you'll return to Nefandus and help her."

Vanessa could feel him softly probing her mind, searching for her answer, pushing her memories aside and scattering her thoughts. But she knew he wouldn't be able to find her decision, because she didn't know yet herself. Jimena had told her that it was too dangerous for her to go back to Nefandus. Should she take the risk? She felt she should, but maybe Stanton had planted that idea in her head.

"Tell me you'll help her," Stanton pleaded.

"Let's just worry about surviving for the next three minutes," Vanessa mumbled; then she heard footsteps rustling through the grass.

She inhaled sharply and clutched Stanton's arm.

A shadow had joined them.

CHAPTER THIRTEEN

VANESSA'S HEART RACED as adrenaline pumped through her. Her survival instinct urged her to run, but Stanton had passed out again and she refused to abandon him. She let her goddess power build, determined to fight the person who stood in the shadows. She hadn't used her power the entire time she had been imprisoned in Nefandus. Like her ability to become invisible, it had been dead inside her. Now the energy grew until the tips of her fingers felt warm and glimmered in the dark.

"You were once brave enough to risk your

soul to save a friend," a voice said from the darkness. Catty stepped forward, her cape settling around her. The smell of the lantern fires in Nefandus still clung to her. "When Karyl, Tymmie, and Cassandra kidnapped me, you defied Maggie and risked everything to save me," she said. "I think you still have the kind of courage needed to return to Nefandus and rescue Serena."

"Like you care," Vanessa said, stumbling backward.

Even though Catty had tried to kill her, Vanessa couldn't bring herself to harm her former friend. She thrust her hands out and released her power. The energy zipped into the night; a bolt of white light that shattered a palm tree. Embers shot into the air, then spiraled down. The cinders landed in the grass and smoldered.

Down the block, porch lights came on, and people stepped outside to see what had caused the noise.

Catty looked surprised. "What's with the fireworks?" she asked, and then her surprise turned into astonishment. "You were getting ready to send me a death blow, weren't you?"

In answer, Vanessa stepped in front of Stanton and shielded him from Catty. "Did you come here to take Stanton back so you could show the Atrox that Stanton's the monk?" Vanessa asked angrily. "Is that your plan, to replace him and become the Princess of Night?"

"Do I look like a princess to you?" Catty smiled mischievously. "I'm dressed all in black, and a princess should definitely wear pink." Then her hand came up and reached for Vanessa's neck.

Vanessa stiffened and squinched her eyes, waiting for the explosion of pain. It never came. She felt a tug around her neck and glanced down. Catty had clasped her moon amulet, but instead of tearing it from her neck, she let the charm fall back into place.

"See?" Catty held up her palm for Vanessa to examine. The skin was unmarked. "I've only been pretending to be a Follower," she said. "If I truly were one, then your moon amulet would have burned my skin."

Vanessa wanted to believe Catty, but she had dealt with many Followers before and knew how skillfully they could lie. Their body language and facial expressions never gave them away.

Still, Vanessa didn't see that scary, predatory gaze in Catty's eyes. Maybe Catty was telling her the truth. But then a recent memory stormed through her mind. "You tried to kill me!" Vanessa shouted.

More porch lights came on and, in the distance, sirens wailed.

"You don't really think I tried to kill you, do you?" Catty looked perplexed, then alarmed. "You do! My act was so good I convinced even you. No wonder my father trusts me."

She looked at Vanessa again, and this time her eyes widened in panic. "I knew you'd fall through a portal before you hit the rocks. Stanton and I planned it! But you and Serena were both supposed to jump before I got there with my father. Stanton, tell her. I don't want her to think that I tried to kill her."

When Stanton didn't respond, Catty glanced

down. He lay, still unconscious, sprawled on the ground.

"Why do you think I got my father away from the cliff as quickly as I could?" Catty asked. "I wanted him to think you were dead so you'd be safe. If he knew you'd passed through a portal, he would have killed me, and then he would have gone looking for you."

Vanessa frowned.

"You have to believe me," Catty said.

But Vanessa still wasn't sure.

"I hated pretending to be a Follower," Catty went on. "You can't imagine what it was like living in Nefandus."

"I was imprisoned in Nefandus," Vanessa said loudly, emphasizing each word. "Serena and I were always terrified."

Catty looked as if she were going to cry, and then she fell against Vanessa and wept. "It was so horrible. I hated every moment of it."

Part of Vanessa wanted to comfort her, but another, stronger, part still couldn't trust her. Vanessa remembered too vividly the smile on

Catty's face when her father ordered her to kill Vanessa.

"Serena and I suffered," Vanessa whispered harshly. "We thought the Atrox had destroyed you, and our grief was——" she interrupted herself with another accusation: "You didn't come to see us and let us know you were okay. You should have told us what had happened."

"I couldn't," Catty choked. "I couldn't tell you the truth, because——"

"The Regulators would have read my thoughts and known that you were a traitor," Vanessa finished for her. "Stanton already told me why he was forced to lie. I suppose you have the same excuse."

"But it's true," Catty said.

"How can I trust you?" Vanessa asked.

"I would have told you if I could have," Catty whispered. "I didn't realize how bad it was for you. Everyone said that the Atrox was taking care of you—that you were unharmed." A sad look crossed her face. "I should have known better than to believe the Atrox's lies."

Only then did Vanessa realize that Catty had been in her mind, reading her thoughts. She touched her temples. "You know how to read minds now?" Vanessa asked.

"I have lots of powers," Catty said. "My father taught me how to use the ones I inherited from him, and the Atrox granted me others."

"If that's supposed to make me trust you, it's not working." Vanessa stared at Catty, remembering how much fun they'd once had together. "I wish we could go back to the way we were before we discovered that we were Daughters of the Moon. It was so much easier just thinking we were freaks."

"No, it wasn't," Catty disagreed. "And even if I did take us back to that time, we'd only have to relive every sorrow that brought us to this moment."

"But there were good times, too," Vanessa said.

Stanton stirred.

"We need your help, Vanessa," Catty said solemnly.

"What do you want me to do?" Vanessa

◄ 121 ►

asked, and immediately wished she hadn't. She knew from the look on Catty's face that they wanted her to do something dangerous.

"Members of the Inner Circle have lost faith in the Atrox," Catty said.

"Good," Vanessa countered.

"All the Followers were surprised when Tianna was able to overcome it," Catty continued.

Maggie had once used a sword to bind the Atrox to its shadow, but over the centuries her binding had weakened. The Atrox had freed itself and had been able to take human form again. But Tianna tricked the Atrox and used the same sword to bind it to its shadow again.

"My father has always wanted to replace the Atrox," Catty went on. "After Tianna deceived it, he was able to convince most of the Followers that the Atrox needed to be deposed."

"You don't expect me to help your father overthrow the Atrox, do you?" Vanessa asked.

"I have something more dangerous in mind," Catty said.

"What?" Vanessa whispered nervously.

"The Atrox senses that there are traitors among the members of the Inner Circle," Catty explained, "and it knows that the black diamond can end its existence. Because of that, it trusts no one, and, at meetings and ceremonies, it spreads its shadow and makes itself too vast for anyone to attack and destroy. A few have tried anyway, but they've only succeeded in injuring the Atrox and, like many Immortals, it can regenerate."

"But what do you want me to do?" Vanessa asked.

"I want you to distract it, make it lose caution and pull itself together, so I can surprise it and destroy it," Catty said.

Vanessa looked up, astounded. "You want me to seduce it so your father can take its place?"

"Stanton will take its place," Catty replied. "He's the Prince of Night."

Hearing his name, Stanton sat up. It was obvious he was still very shaky, but he seemed determined to speak. "Once the Atrox is vanquished, then we can free Serena. Because she is the key, she'll be able to seal the boundary between the two worlds, and Nefandus will no longer be a threat to the world of light."

Vanessa thought for a moment and considered all that they had told her. "But even if I make the Atrox lose caution, you'll still need the black diamond to destroy it."

"I have it," Catty said.

"You do?" Vanessa said. "Show me."

"Later." Catty tilted her head and smiled. "After I have your answer. Are you going to help us or not?"

Vanessa bit her lip, uncertain. "I just don't see how I can tempt the Atrox. Do you really think I'm beguiling enough? Honest answer. Don't just say yes because you're my friend and want me to feel good about myself."

"You're the one person in the world who can seduce the Atrox," Catty said. "It will become reckless if it thinks you've decided to become a Follower."

"Why me?" Vanessa asked even though she feared she already knew the answer.

"The Atrox wants you," Catty replied. "My

father told me that the Atrox has always been with you, watching you grow, waiting for the moment when you discovered that you were a goddess."

"You know about my destiny?" Vanessa asked.

"Everyone in Nefandus does," Stanton mumbled. "Your destiny is the reason the Atrox wouldn't let anyone destroy you."

"And that's why my father wants you dead," Catty said. "He fears that once you become a fallen goddess you'll be too strong, and even the black diamond won't be able to destroy the Atrox."

"You mean I'll protect it?" Vanessa asked, feeling her stomach turn. "That's what the Fates spun for me? I'll become its defender?"

"And more," Catty said softly, looking at Vanessa in the strangest way.

"Jimena told me not to go back to Nefandus," Vanessa said.

"We'll leave as soon as I'm strong enough," Stanton said.

"Won't Regulators be looking for Stanton?" Vanessa asked Catty.

"Before I left, I started a rumor that the monk had fled into the mountains," Catty said. "Regulators will spend days there trying to find him."

"I'll go back to Nefandus with you," Vanessa said uneasily, even though she was certain that both Stanton and Catty had already read her mind.

Terror was a mild word for what she was feeling. She didn't know if she was brave enough to face the Atrox alone, but she had made her decision, and she wouldn't back out now. She glanced up at the fading moon. In any case, she didn't see that she had a choice.

CHAPTER FOURTEEN

VANESSA AND CATTY carried Stanton up the porch steps. A cold breeze swept his hood back. He started shivering. The wind scattered bougainvillea blossoms, and the magenta flowers landed in his hair; he didn't have the strength to brush them away.

"Set him down while I unlock the door." Vanessa pulled the key from her pocket, turned the latch and kicked the door open. Then she grabbed Stanton's ankles again and helped Catty carry him into the living room. Together they lifted him onto the couch.

Vanessa plucked the flowers out of his hair before she hurried back to the door and poked her head outside.

"I don't think anyone followed us." Vanessa closed and locked the door, then switched on a lamp. Her arms and back throbbed painfully, but she was more concerned about Stanton.

He was still shivering, and his chapped lips were constantly moving, seeming to murmur prayers. The words were unintelligible, except for "Serena."

"Should I get him an aspirin, or water, juice maybe?" Vanessa asked Catty. "He doesn't look too good."

"He's immortal." Catty took off her cape and tucked it around him. She wore a long, slinky black dress underneath. "He just needs time to regenerate."

"I hope he can heal himself quickly," Vanessa said. "My birthday is only two days away."

"Everything will be over before you have to make your choice," Catty said, but Vanessa could hear the doubt in her voice. Immediately, her thoughts shifted to Serena, imprisoned alone in Nefandus. She wondered if Stanton were praying for her safety. Vanessa added a prayer of her own.

"You should have appreciated your gift more," Catty scolded, interrupting her. "Won't you miss it?"

"No!" Vanessa said too quickly, and then she relented. "Maybe I should have used it more—"

"To spy on people," Catty said excitedly.

"You would have done that, because you're fearless," Vanessa said. "But I was always afraid of getting into trouble. I wish I hadn't been so afraid."

"You got into trouble anyway." Catty smirked.

"Because of you," Vanessa squealed, and then she smiled, happy to be with her friend again.

"Do you know what you'll choose?" Catty asked.

Vanessa shook her head. "I don't know. Have you decided?"

"My choice was made for me a long time ago," Catty said over her shoulder as she left the living room.

"What does that mean?" Vanessa asked, following her into the kitchen.

Catty ignored her question and slammed through the swinging door. "I'm starved for chocolate!" she yelled. It sounded like a battle cry.

She opened the pantry and began rummaging through the shelves. "Actresses were forever giving your mom big boxes of candy to thank her for making them look so spectacular. So I know there's got to be some chocolate hidden in here."

Catty found a box. When she whipped around to show off her find, the countless photographs of Vanessa taped to the cupboards made her pause.

"Your mom really missed you," Catty said, awestruck. Her eyes darted from one picture to the next. "Does she know you're back?"

"She's in Buffalo with my grandmother." Vanessa glanced at the phone and wondered why she didn't feel like calling her mother. Then, with a breaking heart, she knew. She didn't want to tell her that she was home until after she had survived the next two days. It would be too cruel to call her and then disappear again, perhaps forever this time.

"Kendra moved," Catty said, looking lost. "I wanted to see her, but every time I tried to visit her, I could feel my father or his Regulators drifting behind me. They were probably watching the house, too. I hope they didn't scare Kendra."

"Do you remember how Kendra thought we were aliens from outer space?" Vanessa asked, trying to pull Catty out of her bad mood.

"She was worried that scientists were going to capture us and dissect us to find out how our powers worked," Catty said.

"I was afraid of that, too!" Vanessa shouted.

"I think Kendra was disappointed when I finally told her the truth," Catty said. "She had always dreamed of going to another planet. She sacrificed a lot for me."

Kendra had found Catty walking along the highway in the Arizona desert when Catty was six years old. Kendra had planned to turn her over to the authorities in Yuma. But when Catty made time change, Kendra decided that Catty was an extraterrestrial who had been separated from her parents.

Catty had two memories of the time before that day: one was of a crash, the other of a fire. Kendra believed that both were recollections of the explosion that had occurred when the spacecraft smashed into the ground. She made a decision to protect Catty until her parents could find her, and she kept that promise.

Later, Catty learned that her real mother had abandoned her in order to protect her from her destiny as the heir to the Secret Scroll.

"I miss Kendra," Catty whispered. "If you ever see her again, tell her that I love her."

"Sure." Vanessa took the box of chocolates and opened it. The mouthwatering aroma filled the air. She offered the first choice to Catty.

"As soon as we get back from Nefandus, you can visit her yourself. Better yet, Serena and I will go with you, and then we can lie out on the beach and—" Vanessa stopped speaking. She could hear too much desperation in her voice.

Catty smiled understandingly. She took a

peppermint patty and popped it into her mouth. "Have you seen Michael yet?"

Vanessa blushed and hoped Catty hadn't noticed. She grabbed a chocolate caramel. "What about Kyle? You had such a big crush on him," Vanessa said, changing the subject. "But I always thought you still liked Chris."

"I never stopped liking Chris. How pathetic is that?" Catty snorted and gave Vanessa a chocolate grin. She had purposefully let the chocolate seep from her mouth to gross Vanessa out. She brushed her tongue over her lips. "How can I still like him when I'll never see him again?"

"My mom still loves my dad," Vanessa said. She stuck the candy into her mouth. "That's why she doesn't date."

Vanessa's father had worked as a stunt coordinator for the movies and had been killed in a helicopter accident when she was five years old.

"Sometimes I feel Chris standing beside me, but I know he can't be there," Catty went on. "We all watched him disappear with the Scroll."

"Maybe his spirit is visiting you," Vanessa suggested.

Chris had been the Keeper of the old manuscript called the Secret Scroll. Catty had met him when he gave her the Scroll. As the heir, she was destined to follow the path it described and destroy the Atrox.

But over the centuries, the Scroll had gained power and magic of its own. Chris had feared that it might have the strength to control the heir, so he added a tenth step that instructed the heir to destroy the Scroll before starting on the path. In retaliation, the Scroll bound his life to its existence.

"You had to destroy the Scroll," Vanessa said, sensing Catty's sadness. "Its curse was too dangerous. It had already killed one man, probably more, and its power was growing. You did the right thing."

No heir before Catty had had the courage to destroy the Scroll. But when the fire consumed the manuscript, Chris had vanished with it.

Catty was silent for a long time. "Chris has been visiting me in my dreams." She looked up at

Vanessa to see if she believed her. "I think he's trying to encourage me."

"I'm sure he is," Vanessa soothed.

Catty nodded. "I need encouragement. Every heir has made a fatal error. I wonder what mine will be."

"Maybe you won't make one," Vanessa said, worried for her friend's safety.

Then, with a burst of excitement, Catty asked, "Do you remember how much fun we had at Planet Bang?" She didn't wait for an answer. "Let's go. Please. I feel like getting glammed up and dancing."

"Go," Stanton said grumpily, surprising them both by having regained consciousness. "I need quiet."

"See? Stanton's okay," Catty said. "Let's go have some fun."

Vanessa shook her head. "I might see Michael."

"But you love him," Catty argued.

"Something about me scares him now," Vanessa confessed.

"No way," Catty argued back. "You couldn't

scare him, ever. He's totally in love with you." She grabbed Vanessa's hand. "You're wrong, and I'm going to prove it to you."

Vanessa jerked her hand away. "I'm not going to time-travel. You know how it makes me ill. I don't ever want to go back into that horrible-smelling tunnel. Besides, I know what I saw."

Catty tossed her an impish grin and clamped her fingers around Vanessa's wrist.

"No!" Vanessa yelled, too late.

Incredible power surged through her. A black line appeared in the air behind Catty, and then it spread.

Vanessa stared into the tunnel. "Please, no," she whimpered. She shrieked as they were sucked inside.

The kitchen disappeared in a flash of white light. The opening closed, and they whirled downward. The air felt dry and seemed to bubble. Something foamed around her, but Vanessa never saw anything to account for the tickle.

On all the trips before this one, Catty had always checked the spinning hands on her glow-in-the-dark wristwatch to know when they needed to fall back into time. She couldn't wear a watch now, however, because in Nefandus she had lived with Followers, and they hated timepieces—anything that reminded them of their eternal bond with evil.

Before Vanessa could figure out how Catty would know when to leave the tunnel, they came down in Michael's bedroom. They landed two feet behind him, at the exact moment when Vanessa, in the past, had materialized and fallen from the air.

Vanessa winced as she watched herself thump against the floor. "Ouch!" she said, remembering the pain and humiliation.

Michael swung around, startled by her outcry.

"Catty!" Vanessa squealed. "Do something! He's going to see us!"

Before Michael could turn completely around, Catty whisked Vanessa back into the tunnel.

"He heard you," Catty laughed. "Why did you say anything?"

"I forgot he'd be able to hear me," Vanessa said unhappily. "It's like watching an old video when I see myself in the past. I forget that I'm actually there."

"But now you know that our trip into the past was the reason Michael looked so startled," Catty explained. "*We* scared him, not you, and by the time he could recover, the other you was already running out his bedroom door."

"Maybe," Vanessa said, more concerned about what was happening in front of her.

The tunnel had opened. Vanessa braced herself for a fall, but they alighted gently on the floor.

"You told me once that the only way out of the tunnel was to fall out," Vanessa said, amazed.

"My powers have grown," Catty said.

"Is that because you're a member of the Inner Circle?" Vanessa asked.

Catty didn't answer the question. Instead she playfully nudged Vanessa. "See, I told you Michael was happy to see you."

But Vanessa was no longer worried about

Michael. She was suddenly aware of how miserable Catty must have been in Nefandus. "What was it like living with your father?"

"Horrible." Catty became serious. "I'm ashamed of some of the things I had to do, but I kept reminding myself that I was doing it so I could free you and Serena, and then the three of us could destroy the Atrox."

"What kind of things?

Catty grabbed her hand. "Come on. You have no excuse now. Let's get dressed and go to Planet Bang."

Vanessa hesitated. She didn't feel right about having fun while Serena was suffering in Nefandus.

"You can't wear the dress you're wearing now," Catty said. "It has grass stains and a rip. And there's no way I am going to wear this black Nefandus gown. I look like a witch."

"But what about Stanton?" Vanessa asked, searching for another excuse. "Are you sure it's safe to leave him?

"Go!" he shouted. "I need quiet to recuperate." Already his voice sounded stronger.

"But it's late," Vanessa said.

"Jeez, did you forget how to party?" Catty asked. Then she smiled mysteriously. "Do you remember what Jimena and Serena used to say?"

Vanessa shook her head.

"Non aliquis incipit convivium sine nobis!" Catty shouted. "No one starts the party without us!"

Happiness rushed through Vanessa. *"Nos sumus convivium!"* Vanessa answered. "We are the party!"

They fell against each other, laughing.

"Be quiet!" Stanton groaned.

His outrage made them laugh more. They raced up the stairs, and Vanessa charged into her mother's storage room, Catty close behind her. The air inside still smelled pleasantly of flowers and spice from the perfume that Vanessa had sprayed on earlier.

Catty pulled out a green satin dress with a plunging neckline. She held it against her body and gazed into the mirror.

"Dress to kill," she murmured.

Vanessa caught an odd expression in her

eyes, but when Catty faced her, she was all pixie smiles again.

She pulled out a dress and handed it to Vanessa. "This one is totally daring."

Vanessa took off the dress that Selene had chosen for her earlier and let it fall to the floor. She slipped the new one over her head. The silky material clung to her body. She loved the way the milky white color gave off rainbow reflections, but the V-shaped neckline was too low. "My tattoo shows. What do you think? Should I still wear it?"

"You're totally glamorous," Catty said as she worked the side zipper of her dress. She turned, for Vanessa's approval.

"You'll knock them dead," Vanessa said. The words hung oddly in the air.

"Makeup!" Catty shouted and stepped over to the jars, tubes, and brushes set out on a narrow table.

Vanessa picked up a box of glimmer power and brushed sparkles over her cheeks.

"I've missed drawing." Catty grabbed the

eyeliners, but instead of outlining her eyes, she sat down and drew silver and green flames on her legs. When she was finished, she used a glue stick to make more lines, and while the glue was still wet, she sprinkled it with glitter.

Vanessa pressed iridescent eye shadow on her lid, then smudged it below her eyes.

When they finished, they stood together and stared at their reflections in the mirror.

"We look like mysterious creatures of the night," Catty whispered. "Something from a fairy tale."

"Goddess warriors," Vanessa breathed.

"Dangerous beauties," Catty sighed.

"I love you, Catty," Vanessa said with a sudden burst of emotion. "You're the best friend I've ever had."

"Quit with the gooey stuff," Catty joked. Then her face became serious. "I love you, too. If you weren't here my life would have been a lot harder."

"Ditto," Vanessa said. "Friends forever."

"Forever," Catty whispered back. She stretched

◄ 142 ►

her arms over her head and, with a dreamy smile, swayed her hips before spinning out of the room. She rushed down the hallway.

Vanessa ran after her.

Their high heels struck the wooden stairs as they descended. The clatter roused Stanton again.

"Would you get out of here?" he yelled. "I need sleep to regenerate."

As Catty reached for the doorknob, Vanessa saw a circle of red, swollen skin on the inside of her arm. She caught Catty's wrist and turned her arm over to examine the welts. The Phoenix crest had been branded into Catty's skin.

Vanessa looked at her friend. "Catty, how did you earn the Phoenix crest?"

"Truth?" The grief-stricken expression on Catty's face made Vanessa shudder.

"Truth," Vanessa answered.

"I killed Kyle," Catty confessed.

CHAPTER FIFTEEN

CATTY LEANED AGAINST the washing machine and stared out the window. Wind rushed through the trees, bending the branches. The shadows slid back and forth over her face.

"Kyle had been looking for me," Catty began. "I knew it was dangerous for him to see me. I tried to warn him away. I even left a note for him once, when he went over to Kendra's house. She had moved by then, but he was desperate to find me, and he questioned the new owner."

"I remember Kyle was the one who took you

into Nefandus to meet your father," Vanessa put in.

Catty nodded. "I thought he was just a *servus*, a slave, who had escaped Nefandus, but then I learned about the Legend."

"What legend?" Vanessa asked.

"The Legend of the Four," Catty answered, and then she began reciting softly, "Four will come together and mend what evil has done. Then as brothers, they will make a journey into evil's land and find the black diamond, with which they will fulfill their destiny. Four will venture in, but only one will venture out."

"Kyle was one of the Four?" Vanessa asked.

Catty nodded. "When I found out that he was one of the Four of Legend, I knew I had to contact him, because I had the black diamond. I felt that Kyle and his three friends were my only hope. I didn't know then that my father still didn't trust me. Looking back, I know I should have waited, but I was desperate. I wanted to free you and Serena." She looked at Vanessa. "Talk was growing about forcing you into the cold fire. I knew Serena would become a fallen goddess, but unless the Atrox invited you in . . ." Her words fell away.

"I know," Vanessa said. She didn't need to hear the explanation again.

Catty's voice dropped to a thin whisper. "I met Kyle and his friends in Nefandus. We made plans for attacking the Atrox and destroying it, but when we started to leave, my father and his Regulators surrounded us."

"How did you escape?" Vanessa asked.

"We didn't," Catty answered. "They kept us trapped while they summoned the Atrox. I think my father was planning to turn all five of us over to the Atrox. But Kyle came up with a plan." She waited until the quivering in her chin stopped. Then she went on, "Kyle realized we were defeated. He spoke to his friends, and all three, Berto, Obie, and Samuel, agreed with him. They gathered around me and told me that when the Atrox arrived, I had to pretend that I had captured them."

"They wanted you to turn them over to the Atrox?" Vanessa asked.

"That wasn't what they *wanted*," Catty said, "but we were cornered. They figured that if I could convince the Atrox that I had captured the Four of Legend, then I would prove my loyalty to the ancient evil and maybe then I would be able to destroy it. Otherwise—"

"No one would have been left," Vanessa said, "because Serena and I were still imprisoned."

"And it would have had the black diamond, too," Catty added.

"How did you hide the black diamond?" Vanessa asked.

"When I turned Kyle and his friends over, the Atrox was so elated that it never asked about the diamond," Catty explained.

"They sacrificed their lives so we could destroy the Atrox," Vanessa whispered.

"Not just their lives," Catty said, correcting her, and then she continued her story. "So I marched them out to the Atrox. I had to keep my mind blank, my emotions cold." Catty lifted her head and gazed into Vanessa's eyes. "Have you ever seen what a Regulator does to destroy an immortal *servus*?"

Vanessa shook her head.

"My father's favorite Regulator came forward. He grabbed Kyle and slammed him against his chest. Kyle didn't scream, even though the pain must have been excruciating," Catty said.

"What happened to him?" Vanessa asked.

"The Regulator absorbed Kyle into his body, and all that remained of Kyle was a few drops of blood on the Regulator's chest. Then, as a final test of my loyalty, the Regulator stepped in front of me. I knew my father was watching me, and that when I looked up I would see something horrible."

"And?" Vanessa asked.

"I saw Kyle looking back at me through the Regulator's eyes," Catty said, "but there was no sadness in his expression. Even then, he was warning me to keep my emotions hidden. At least, that's what I sensed he was telling me. I wanted to scream, but I managed to laugh instead."

Bile rose in Vanessa's throat. She breathed

through her mouth, trying to calm her stomach.

"Then Berto, Samuel, and Obie were each absorbed," Catty said.

"You didn't kill Kyle," Vanessa said firmly. "You're definitely not responsible for what happened."

"I am," Catty insisted. "I never should have contacted him. I knew the risk."

"But still," Vanessa whispered. "You can't blame yourself."

"That's how I won the Phoenix crest," Catty said quietly.

After a moment, Vanessa spoke, "We have to go dancing."

"No, you were right. Maybe it's not such a good idea," Catty answered.

Vanessa grabbed a dishcloth and wiped away the mascara that had run down Catty's cheeks.

"We can't concentrate on things that will make us feel more fear," Vanessa warned. "If we stay here and focus on all the bad things that the Atrox and your father have done, we'll lose our courage, and then the battle. Even a moment's hesitation could cost us everything when we fight the Atrox; you know that."

"You're right," Catty agreed, but she continued to stare out the window. At last, she turned and faced Vanessa. "Let's have some fun," she said. "And when we're ready, we'll destroy the Atrox, for Kyle and his friends."

"And for Maggie and Tianna," Vanessa added.

Catty nodded. "And for Serena," she said solemnly.

A chill rushed through Vanessa. Catty already thought that Serena was dead, or at least fallen. Vanessa was overcome with guilt. If she had had the courage to jump off the cliff, Serena would have been there with her now. But she would not let herself cry. Maggie had told them that the Daughters were an unstoppable force; their breed was descended from invincible warriors. She stepped boldly forward, determined to remember the courage of the Daughters who had come before her and honor them with her bravery.

Holding her head high, she left through the back door, the night wind rushing around her.

CHAPTER SIXTEEN

WITH ARMS LINKED, Vanessa and Catty strolled down the sidewalk, the tapping of their heels echoing behind them. When they neared Planet Bang, the music from inside pulsed around them with a steady thump.

"I am so ready to dance." Vanessa leaned against Catty. "I've missed just going out with my friends."

Catty swayed her hips against Vanessa and laughed. "Me, too. My dad made me date some real creeps in Nefandus. I think he wanted me to hook up with a demon." Catty giggled, but there was too much sadness in her laugh.

"Remember the time we—" Vanessa stopped. Her moon amulet throbbed against her chest, warning her of danger. She slowed her steps and studied the deeper shadows beneath the trees, but she didn't see any spectral forms gliding in the dark.

Catty ran up to the corner and waited for her. "The Followers aren't hiding," she said. "They're reckless now, because they think they've won. Come see."

Vanessa joined Catty. Her heart had already found a faster rhythm. She looked down the street and gasped.

Outside Planet Bang, Followers had gathered. Dozens of them had clustered in small groups on the sidewalk and in the street, talking, laughing, and drinking beer. Some were dancing, their bodies tight against one another. A few were taunting the kids who waited on line to go inside.

Two security guards marched back and forth, trying to stop the fights that were breaking out.

The smell of clove cigarettes and musky perfumes was as strong as the tension in the air.

"There are way too many Followers," Vanessa said. "Maybe we should go back to my house and wait there for Stanton to get well."

"No way," Catty answered. "They're not stopping me."

"But—"

"I'll take care of it," Catty assured her. "Don't show any fear."

"Right," Vanessa agreed, but already her anxiety was rising, and her stomach was twisting into knots. She could feel the cold sweat of fear prickling her temples. She clutched her moon amulet, hoping it would calm her. "How are we going to walk past all of them?"

"Just do what I do." Catty walked ahead as if she owned the night. She was already lost in the crowd before Vanessa had summoned even enough courage to take her first step.

Vanessa took a deep breath and started forward. She tried to walk with the same flirty swing as Catty, but her frayed nerves made her feet feel shaky in the stiletto heels. Her ankle wobbled, and she stumbled.

A Follower wearing a long coat caught her. The glow from her moon amulet lit his face, and his eyes flickered with yellow light. Scars nicked his cheeks in a lattice pattern.

"Vanessa," he whispered with delight. "The last Daughter of the Moon."

She could sense his desire. He waggled his tongue at her. The silver tongue rings reflected the light from the flashing neon sign outside Planet Bang.

Her body tensed with power as she prepared to defend herself. But when he touched her shoulder, the energy immediately drained from her. That had never happened before. He laughed, enjoying her confusion. His gaze dropped lower and lingered on her chest. She wished she hadn't worn such a low-cut dress.

"Nice tattoo," he murmured as he stroked her collarbone with his thumb.

Her heart stuttered and she couldn't breathe. His boldness frightened her, and his touch made her shudder. He whispered her name again, per-versely excited by her fear.

She pulled away from him and bumped into Karyl.

"You can't outrun us now," Karyl sneered. "We rule."

His shirt was open, showing off his hard-packed muscles, and his arm was draped around a girl with spiderwebs tattooed over her neck and chest. She stared at Vanessa through thick black bangs.

"Goddess," she hissed, "you lost. Maybe I'll let you be my pet after the final eclipse."

The Followers standing nearby laughed.

A tall girl with a model's perfect face poked a finger into Vanessa's side. "All the goody girls are dancing inside."

Vanessa hunched her shoulders and pulled her arms close to her body, trying to slip around the last group of Followers. She dropped her chin and stared down at the ground to avoid eye contact.

Catty came back to her and took her arm.

"Why are you letting them intimidate you?" she scolded. "Strut your stuff. You're more powerful than any of them."

"A guy just drained my power," Vanessa argued. "This is really creepy. Why don't they attack?"

"Because they're afraid of you," Catty whispered.

"They are?" Vanessa glanced back. The Followers were glaring at her. She didn't sense any fear in their frowns. "What makes you think they are?"

"Keep up with me." Catty started off again, not answering her question. "You'll feel better once we're inside."

Vanessa hurried after Catty; suddenly Tymmie stepped in front of her, fiery anticipation in his eyes. He squeezed her against him.

"Nice dress," he whispered against her cheek. "Did you wear it for me?"

Vanessa struggled to pull away from him, but that only made him laugh.

"I knew you couldn't stay away from me," he

teased. "In the new world, after the eclipse, you'll want to hook up with me. So why wait?" He started to dematerialize, taking her with him.

"Catty!" Vanessa yelled, too nervous to focus her power. There was nothing warrior about her now. She was starting to disappear and couldn't fight the change taking place inside her. Already her fingers were shadows. She wasn't the unstoppable force that Maggie had declared; she was nothing more than a scared, whimpering girl.

CHAPTER SEVENTEEN

SOMEONE RAMMED into Tymmie's back, causing him to drop his hold on Vanessa. When he let go of her, cold spasms shuddered through her as her body became solid again. Tymmie spun around.

"The goddess is mine," the guy with the tuft of hair said before he slugged Tymmie.

The security guards ran toward them, but Catty was quicker. She threw herself between Tymmie and the other guy.

Blood trickled from Tymmie's nose.

"Vanessa is with me," Catty warned. "I'm taking her back to Nefandus as a present for my dad. Does anyone want to fight over her now?"

Tymmie backed away and faded into a fragment of night that sped up the side of the stucco wall.

The Follower with the tuft of hair bowed and ambled back to his group.

Abruptly, the two security guards stopped.

"Damned fires," the larger one said. "The smoke makes me think I'm seeing ghosts."

"You're not the only one. Things keep getting weirder every day," the shorter guard added. "I'll be glad when they finally get the fires under control."

They sauntered away, thumbs hooked in their utility belts.

"Tymmie obviously didn't know you were with me." Catty held Vanessa's hand and tried to calm her, but Vanessa's trembling didn't go away all at once.

"Remember he was an *infidus*?" Catty asked.

"One of the Followers loyal to Lambert who

◄ 1 5 9 ►

wanted to overthrow the Atrox," Vanessa said.

"He's still an *infidus*, but loyal to my father now," Catty said. "None of them will bother us again, because they know they'll have to answer to my father if they do."

"Does your father know I'm not dead?" Vanessa asked.

"You still don't trust me, do you?" Catty grinned. "I'm not taking you back to my father, but it's safer if they think I am."

"But what if one of them goes back and tells him that we're together?" Vanessa asked, wondering if Catty might still be deceiving her.

"Why would any of them do that?" Catty looked truly baffled. "I wear the Phoenix crest. They won't question me." She pulled Vanessa forward. "Come on. We came here to dance, and that's what we're going to do."

"I have a really bad feeling about this," Vanessa mumbled. "It's just like before, when we were going to La Brea High. You were always making me do things I didn't want to do, and we always ended up getting in trouble."

"I know," Catty answered smugly. "But didn't it make your life more fun?"

Vanessa sighed and reluctantly nodded. "But it wasn't dangerous then."

As they neared the entrance to Planet Bang, the music grew louder and vibrated through them. Vanessa breathed in the heady mix of perfume and aftershave, and her spirits started to rise again. She wanted to dance and forget all her worries.

"Watch this." Catty led Vanessa past the kids standing behind the metal barriers. Then she cut to the front of the line, ignoring the shouts and protests from the kids behind them. Her eyes dilated, and she stared at the guard.

He scratched his forehead as if he could feel Catty inside his head. Then he smiled. "Didn't I just check you two?"

"Yes," Catty said sweetly.

"What are you waiting for, then?" He waved them through. "Go on in."

"We didn't even have to pay the entrance fee," Catty said excitedly.

Vanessa grabbed Catty's arm before they went inside. "Look," she whispered, alarmed, and pointed up at the night sky.

The red glow that had rimmed the moon was fading.

"Maybe we should go back to Nefandus without Stanton," Vanessa suggested.

"What good would it do?" Catty asked. "We need him."

"Why?" Vanessa asked.

Instead of answering, Catty pulled at the back of Vanessa's dress. "Come on. Let's dance."

Catty ran inside. Vanessa skipped after her. Together they pushed their way into the dark, crowded room. Red lasers cut across the smoke rising from the machines, and the beat of the drums vibrated through them.

Vanessa closed her eyes and danced, feeling the music become part of her. Her body began to relax, and gradually her worries left her. When the song ended, she didn't stop dancing. She kept her eyes closed and swayed, her hands above her head, not wanting the moment to end.

The music started again, and Vanessa immediately recognized the short, repeated phrase of
chords played on the guitar. She opened her eyes
and turned around. Her heart skipped a beat.

Michael stood on the stage. He had come to
Planet Bang after all. He pressed his lips against
the mike and sang the song he had been compos-
ing when she had materialized in his room.

Catty elbowed her. "That song is about you!"

"I hope it is," Vanessa said dreamily. If it
was, then it meant Michael loved her as deeply as
she loved him.

"Vanessa!" Corrine screamed and ran up to
her, destroying the moment. "I'm so glad you
came back."

"Catty!" Jessica and Melanie squealed together,
jumping up and down.

"Great." Catty leaned against Vanessa.
"These are not the people I want to spend time
with before we go back to Nefandus. Come on,"
she said, leading the way.

Catty and Vanessa ducked behind a couple
who were kissing, and pretended not to hear

Corrine calling after them. They jostled around swinging hands and kicking feet trying to get away, but Corrine pushed after them.

"Catty, did you join the circus, too?" Corrine asked when at last she caught up to them

"What?" Catty's mouth dropped open. Her eyes widened, and she looked at Vanessa for an explanation.

"Sorry." Vanessa shrugged and smiled guiltily. "I had to tell her something after I got upset and vanished in front of her."

"But, the circus?" Catty started giggling. "Couldn't you think of something better? Does she think I was a clown? She couldn't have believed you."

Corrine shoved between them and linked her arms with theirs. "Fess up. I want all the details. Were you a magician's assistant, too?"

"I guess you could say I lived in a world of magic," Catty said, unlinking her arm from Corrine's. She pressed her body in between two guys and started dancing with them.

Melanie and Jessica joined them.

"We've told everyone," Melanie said, "even Michael. I can't believe you joined . . ."

Catty narrowed her eyes, and Melanie touched her forehead. "I lost my train of thought." But her confusion lasted only for a second. She glanced at Vanessa and screeched, "You got a tattoo!"

"Let me see." Corrine traced her fingers over the tattoo on Vanessa's chest. "I never thought you'd do something like that. It feels bumpy. Is it just a tattoo?"

Vanessa brushed Corrine's hand away, suddenly self-conscious. She glanced up at the stage. She wasn't going to waste any more time with Corrine. She wanted to be with Michael.

"The tattoo looks good." Derek joined them and smiled broadly. He couldn't take his eyes off Catty. "Where'd you learn how to dance like that?" he asked.

"Boarding school," Catty lied.

"Boarding school," Corrine repeated. Her head snapped around, and she glared at Vanessa. "I thought you said you joined the circus."

"Get real, Corrine," Catty answered, and then she glanced back at Derek. "Dance with me."

He placed his hands on Catty's hips and followed her lead.

"She's turned out to be just like Tianna," Corrine huffed. She turned on Vanessa. "I don't know how you can have friends like Catty. You're so much better."

Melanie and Jessica nodded in agreement. They each pulled out a gloss from their pockets and rubbed pink color over their lips.

"Catty is the best friend anyone could ever have," Vanessa snapped before she stole away from them and worked her way closer to the stage.

Kids she recognized from school stopped dancing, surprised to see her. Some hugged her. Others kissed her. They all wanted to know what had happened to her. She appreciated their concern, but right now she didn't have time to talk. She had only one goal in mind.

She stared up at Michael and listened to his song.

When Michael glanced out at the audience,

he stopped singing and took off his guitar. He set it aside, then jumped off the stage and shoved his way toward her.

He stopped a short distance from her, and her heart fell. He stood in front of Corrine and smiled down at her. What was he saying to her? The hands that should have been embracing Vanessa touched Corrine's shoulders. So Michael had found someone else after all. No wonder Corrine had said such nice things about him.

Heartbroken, Vanessa turned to leave. She elbowed her way through the dancers. Catty could stay and dance and have her party, but Vanessa was going to go home, sit by Stanton's side, and sulk.

VANESSA HAD ALMOST reached the door when someone touched her back. She wasn't going to let Catty stop her this time.

"I'm going home, Catty," she said belligerently as she swung around.

Michael stared down at her. "Corrine told me that you were here," he said. "I'm glad I caught you before you left."

She glanced behind him to see if Corrine was waiting for him. He turned and followed her gaze. "Are you looking for Catty?" he asked.

She shook her head. She loved the way he was looking at her.

"I'm sorry I acted so weird when you came over to my house," Michael said.

"I should have called you before I came over," Vanessa said, "but I was just so crazy to see you."

"I missed you, too," he said.

He touched her gently, as if he weren't sure if she would accept his embrace. His fingers slid over her arm, and she caught her breath.

She inched closer. "Where's Corrine?"

"I don't know." He eased closer. "I didn't go out with anyone else while you were gone."

"You didn't hook up with Corrine?" she asked, praying that he hadn't.

He shook his head. "She's just a friend. She could never replace you."

"I didn't see anyone, either," Vanessa said, even though that would have been an impossibility for her. Still, she wanted Michael to know that she had never stopped caring for him.

"Can you stay a little while longer?" he asked.

She nodded and let him lead her back to the dance floor. She started dancing near him. Her body moved sinuously and slowly. She felt the roughness of his jeans against her thigh. Her breath quickened. She dropped her hands and let them rest on his chest.

When Michael leaned down and kissed her, waves of desire rose inside her.

"You're going to run away again, aren't you?" He nuzzled her neck. "I can see it in your eyes. You've got a faraway, sad look. Why do you have to leave?"

"I have to go, and I might never come back," she said against his ear. "I can't tell you more than that. I wish I could, but you wouldn't believe me even if I did."

He held her tighter. "But it doesn't have anything to do with a circus or a magician, does it?"

She shook her head, then pulled back, looked up into his eyes, and bit her lip.

"What?" he coaxed. "I know you have something more that you want to tell me. You only bite your lip like that when you're afraid to say what's on your mind."

"Is your van here?" she asked as a blush rose to her cheeks.

"Do you want me to take you home?" He looked disappointed.

"No, I want . . ." she stopped. "Don't make me say the words. I don't think I can."

His face brightened as he understood. "My van's parked in back." He took her hand and guided her around the dancers to an exit behind the stage.

He held the door open, and she stepped outside into the cool night air. The alley was dark except for a flickering security light that buzzed noisily at the entrance. She didn't sense any Followers hiding in the shadows.

Michael stepped over to his van and slid the side door open. "Are you sure?" he asked.

She nodded, a pleasant ache of anticipation rushing through her.

He pulled her against him and kissed her once more. Her desire was stronger than ever. He crawled into the van, pushed his surfboard aside, and spread a sleeping bag on the floor. When he was finished, he held out his hand and guided her inside. His fingers brushed over her waist as he helped her sit down. Then he took off her shoes and set them aside. He removed his shirt before he closed the van door.

Kneeling, they faced each other and embraced.

After their second kiss, Michael gently lowered her onto the sleeping bag. His hand slipped under her dress and rested on her stomach.

As Michael started to kiss her, the van door slid open with a harsh rasp of metal.

CHAPTER NINETEEN

STANTON LEANED INTO the van, his hands braced against the roof. Once again, he exuded an aura of irresistible charm and danger. A black shirt and jeans had replaced his monk's robe. His blond hair hung down in his eyes, and the clean smell of soap clung to him, as if he had just taken a shower.

Michael rolled over, then jackknifed into a sitting position. "Stanton," he snarled.

"Hey, Michael." Stanton stepped back and

grinned maliciously. "Did I catch you at a bad time?"

"What is it with you? Are you some kind of pervert?" Michael jumped out of the van. "You stalked us on our first date and ruined that evening. Have you been following us ever since so you could ruin this moment, too?" He lifted his head and thrust out his jaw.

Stanton ignored Michael's threatening pose and turned to Vanessa. "Come on," he said. "We have to leave now."

"Stay there, Vanessa," Michael ordered. "I'll take care of this chump."

"Chump?" Stanton said, turning his attention back to Michael. "Did you call me a chump?"

"I have to go with him." Vanessa started out of the van.

"Is he the magician you ran off with?" Michael asked with unpleasant anger. "I didn't see him hanging around with all his badass friends the entire time you were gone. Was he with you?"

"You shouldn't be so jealous of me, Michael," Stanton soothed, obviously enjoying Michael's frustration and rage. "I thought you'd gotten over that a long time ago."

"Calm down, Michael," Vanessa warned. "You don't want to fight him. Remember what you told me? You said he always tries to goad you into a fight. Don't give him what he wants."

Michael lunged, but Stanton stepped aside; Michael kept moving forward, his feet slapping the pavement. He caught himself and twisted around to face Stanton again.

Vanessa scrambled out of the van and pinched Stanton's arm. "Please, don't hurt him."

"I can beat this punk." Michael scowled and charged Stanton again. This time Stanton didn't move. In a flash, he turned into a shadow as Michael's fist swished through him. Then, immediately, Stanton materialized again, the transformation so quick that even Vanessa thought his disappearance had been an illusion.

"What the—?" Michael stared down at his fingers, then back at Stanton.

Vanessa could feel the power building inside Stanton. "Please don't hurt him, Stanton!" she screamed. "Please!"

"Too late," Stanton answered.

Michael froze, entranced. His eyes lost their brightness.

"What did you do to him?" Vanessa asked, rubbing Michael's arm. His skin felt cold and wet.

"He'll come out of it in a few minutes," Stanton said.

"How will I ever explain this to him?" Vanessa asked.

"I already have," Stanton answered. "When the trance releases him, he's going to think that he and I had a really long conversation and that I took you home so he could have some time to readjust his attitude, put a little romance into his thinking."

"And what did you say in your really long conversation?" Vanessa asked as she started walking down the alley with Stanton.

"He'll tell you," Stanton said. "I'm sure he will. I don't think he's really that stupid, even though he acts like it at times."

"I really like him, Stanton," Vanessa said. "I hope you didn't ruin it for me."

"You'll thank me someday," Stanton said. "He'll know better next time. I can't believe you were in the back of his van like some hoochie mama."

"That's what I wanted," Vanessa said, trying to keep up with Stanton's fast pace. "I'm probably going to die before the night is over."

She stopped. Her fear had finally been spoken. "I wanted to know what it felt like before I died," she confessed and fell into Stanton's arms.

"I'll make sure you survive this night," Stanton whispered as he patted her on the back. "But then you have to promise me that you'll wait until you can have moonlight and a bed of rose petals."

"Is that what this is about?" She pulled back so she could look into his eyes. "You didn't think the moment was romantic enough?"

"It wasn't—but that's not the reason I had to

find you," he said solemnly. "Time has run out. We have to go back to Nefandus now." He nodded toward the sky.

Vanessa gazed up at the black, endless night. The moon had vanished.

CHAPTER TWENTY

VANESSA CAST ONE last look back at Michael and sighed.

"You'll see him again." Stanton tugged at her arm. "We have to find Catty now and leave."

"Be safe," Vanessa whispered back at Michael. Then she turned and ran after Stanton, her bare feet smacking against the cold concrete.

The music from inside Planet Bang grew fainter as they hurried down the street. By the time they reached the next block, the soughing of the wind through the trees had become louder than the thumping beat.

A few minutes later they found Catty. She stood beneath the drooping branches of a shrub that twined up the side of a house.

"Go get her," Stanton said impatiently. He waited near the curb, vigilantly watching the shadows.

Vanessa stepped across the lawn. The lush scent of honeysuckle drifted over her. She breathed in the fragrance and filled her lungs with the luxurious aroma. "Why aren't you dancing? I thought that's how you wanted to spend—" Vanessa interrupted herself. She had almost said, "your last night."

"My feet got tired." Catty kicked out her foot. She had taken off the ankle-breaking heels and wore only her toe rings now. In the dim light, Vanessa could see the blister on the side of her big toe.

Catty picked a blossom and sipped the nectar from the end. When she was finished, a serene expression covered her face. "The blossoms collect the moonbeams and store them in the nectar."

Vanessa snapped off a branch and brushed the soft petals across her cheek.

"The goddess who reared Tianna fed her honeysuckle nectar," Catty explained. "It was the magic elixir she used to give Tianna a soul. I use it to give myself courage."

"I've never tried it before." Vanessa took a flower, pinched off the end, then held her head back and let the sugary liquid drop on her tongue. Even though the moon was gone, she could feel its magic race through her.

"When the moon is full, the nectar tastes sweeter." Catty tore off another sprig of blossoms. She dropped it and looked down. "I'm scared, Vanessa," she confessed quietly. "So scared."

"Me, too," Vanessa replied.

"I hope we're doing the right thing," Catty whispered. "It's hard to know without Maggie to guide us."

"I think we are," Vanessa said. "We're the

only hope the world has left. We can't let the Atrox win."

"No, I mean me and Stanton. Should we be taking you back with us?" Catty asked. "It's so risky. Maybe we should go alone and do our best to catch the Atrox."

Vanessa touched Catty's arm. "I know it's dangerous," she said. "But we have to try. This is what we were born to do. We're the Daughters of the Moon."

Catty's lip trembled, and she looked as if she were trying to say something difficult.

"What is it?" Vanessa asked.

"If something happens—"

"We're going to beat the Atrox," Vanessa said firmly, even though she didn't feel certain that they could. The words *die trying* kept coming to her mind.

Catty smiled weakly and went on, "But if something does happen, I want you to know that all those times I got you into trouble, it was never malicious, even the times when you ended up on restriction because of me. I just wanted you to have more fun. You were always acting so serious and following the rules, even the stupid ones."

"I know you never did it to be mean," Vanessa said. "Why are you so worried about that now?"

"I just wanted you to know. That's all." Catty frowned and looked away.

"What aren't you telling me?" Vanessa asked. "We've been friends a long time, and I know you're holding something back."

Before Catty could answer, Stanton stepped between them.

"We need to leave now," he said, his eyes narrowed and serious. He grasped Catty's hand, and then he clenched Vanessa's fingers.

Vanessa understood what he was going to do. She took a deep breath. She wouldn't be able to breathe again until they were in Nefandus. Something inside her collapsed, and she cried out for him to stop.

"Too late," he whispered in a tense voice. "I can't."

Vanessa sensed that she would never see Los Angeles again and she hadn't had a chance to say good-bye. She loved the city: Melrose Avenue and Pink's, the Beverly Center and Farmers Market, the beaches and palm trees. She'd even miss the traffic sounds and the paparazzi.

Before she was ready, the night buckled. The neighborhood of stucco houses disappeared, and a veil descended over her. Her body lost all sense of feeling while her molecules rearranged. She tried to concentrate on the soft, continuous *Om* rather than on what awaited her in Nefandus. When the numbness left her, she stepped forward and was surprised to find herself in a frilly, overdecorated bedroom.

Catty and Stanton were already pacing near a bed that was covered with a pink satin comforter and had lacy pillows thrown on top. They stopped when they saw her.

Vanessa sensed their urgency. They looked worried. She caught her own reflection in the mirror over the dressing table and quickly looked away. She hated the terror she saw in her eyes.

"The Atrox won't be able to find you in this room." Stanton clenched his jaw.

"Don't leave until we get back," Catty ordered.

"Wait! Don't we need to have a plan?" Vanessa asked. She hadn't thought they would leave her alone so quickly. "Where are you going?"

Stanton and Catty glanced at each other, each waiting for the other to answer.

"We need to find the right place to ambush the Atrox," Stanton said finally.

"A place where you can use me as bait," Vanessa joked. Fear made her stutter, and the words came out wrong. The seriousness of what they were about to do settled over them, and they became deadly quiet.

Stanton studied Vanessa with something close to pity in his eyes. Finally, he interrupted the silence and spoke, "I love Serena. That's why I'm taking this risk." Then he slammed his hand against the wall.

His sudden motion made Vanessa jump.

A hidden panel within the stone wall scraped open, revealing a hallway on the other side.

Stanton left the room and stepped out into the vast corridor.

Catty hugged Vanessa. "Good-bye," she said, and then she tossed Vanessa one of her impish, Catty grins. But her farewell hung ominously in the air, and Vanessa could sense her nervousness.

"Catty, wait," Vanessa said. "We've been friends forever, and I know there's something you're not telling me."

"Don't be silly," Catty replied. She turned and hurried out of the room.

Vanessa felt certain that she had seen tears in Catty's eyes. She rushed after her, but the panel closed in front of her with the grinding sound of stone gnashing over stone. Vanessa was left alone in the room, her uneasiness growing. Her legs felt too weak, her arms too jittery, to continue standing. She sat down on the tufted bench at the foot of the bed.

She tried not to think of where she was and what she had to do. Instead, she focused on Michael and wondered what would have happened if Stanton hadn't opened the van door.

She imagined Michael's arms around her again, his soft touch, his gentle kiss.

A sharp sound roused her from her fantasy. She listened, her nerves thrumming.

Someone was on the other side of the wall. She waited for Catty and Stanton to open the hidden panel and join her.

The knocking continued. The sound set her on edge.

Maybe she had to do something to unlock the secret passageway from her side. She walked over to the wall and traced her fingers over the stones where Stanton had struck his hand. She didn't see a lever or handle, or anything to push that would make the stone wall move.

Whoever was on the other side of the wall continued knocking, with a light, teasing tap.

"Catty?" she said.

"Vanessa." The harsh, eerie whisper that answered made her reel back. She felt a primal urge to run, but the room had no windows, no doors, no way out. She was trapped.

She continued backing up until her shoulders hit the opposite wall.

"No," she whimpered, repeating the word. This couldn't be. But even as she tried to deny it, the truth was hammering through her. Catty and Stanton had deceived her after all. Their friendship had been a lie, their concern, their smiles, all of it a deception that she had believed. Why had she been so gullible?

At last, the hidden panel slid open.

The Atrox seeped into the room, a solid mass of black shadow, different from the shadows of shape-shifters. This shadow roiled and grew, only to fall back into itself before stretching out again.

She could feel its eagerness, its need. And then with the pain of a piercing headache, she felt it in her mind. Her stomach turned.

When the Atrox found her anger at Catty and Stanton for their deception, it pulled out of her mind again, satisfied. "Your friends betrayed you, and they did it well."

"I hate them for it," Vanessa said miserably,

but she didn't want to hate them, especially not Catty. She felt hurt. How could they do this to her?

The Atrox curled around her. Its touch aroused intense disgust within her.

"Sweet goddess," it said. "I will reward Catty and Stanton for bringing you back to me. You will honor them as well when you see the future that I will give you. You'll have the riches of both worlds, anything you desire."

"Please, just let me go," Vanessa pleaded. "All I've ever wanted was just to be like everyone else. I can't hurt you. I'm no threat. If you could see how hard I have to try, you wouldn't want me anyway. I've always been too cautious, always choosing to do what's right and sensible and expected. I won't even know how to use all those riches, and as an evil goddess I'll be a complete failure."

She stopped rambling. It was a waste of time. The Atrox didn't care. Her chest heaved, and she pressed her fingers over her eyes, fighting back tears. There wasn't time to cry. She had to convince the Atrox to let her go.

"You've won," she said at last. "The moon is already dead. Why do you need me as well?"

"Because you alone can ensure the final eclipse," it murmured, and then, with the softness of a warm breeze, it caressed her.

▼

CHAPTER TWENTY-ONE

"I WON'T," VANESSA answered defiantly through her fear. She clutched her moon amulet with both hands. "I refuse to help you bring about the final eclipse."

The Atrox chuckled in response. "Sweet goddess, why are you fighting me?"

She twisted around, trying to see a glimmer of light in the darkness, anything that would show her a way to escape the Atrox, but its blackness had completely enshrouded her.

She fell to her knees, still holding tightly on to the charm. Even if she did find a way to escape the Atrox, and then this room, what chance did she have of reaching a portal? And if she managed, by some miracle, to get back to Los Angeles, what could she do then? She had no place to go where she would be safe. For a moment, she thought about Jimena, but her plan to hide had been too hasty. It wouldn't have worked, either.

"You shouldn't feel like such a victim," the Atrox whispered. "That role doesn't become you. You're destined for greatness, infamy. Everyone will know of your wickedness and bow to you."

"That's not something I want!" she cried.

Tendrils formed within the shadow and lifted her, forcing her to stand, and then, with tenderness, wiped the tears from her cheeks. Each touch made a spasm rush through her. She felt too dizzy to remain on her feet. The Atrox held her up, but she would not let it take her hands away from her moon amulet.

"Souls choose their own destiny before birth," the Atrox said, "and then they go before Lachesis, one of the sisters of Fate."

"I would never choose this," Vanessa countered. "It's not in me. I can't be the reason for the final eclipse."

"But Lachesis wove your destiny, and once that is done, your fate is irrevocable. No one can alter her decree, not even Selene," the Atrox assured her.

Vanessa tried to concentrate. The Atrox had to be lying to her. Maggie would have foreseen something this catastrophic and would have warned her.

"Lachesis gives each soul a guardian angel," the Atrox continued.

"Then where is mine?" Vanessa demanded.

"Embracing you," the Atrox answered.

"You?" Vanessa asked. "How did you protect me?"

"Remember the shadow in your room at night," the Atrox asked, "the one that grew and stretched?"

"My mother told me it was my imagination . . ." Her words fell away. The shadow had frightened her, and now she understood why. "You were the shadow in the darkness that scared me?"

"It was always me, watching you grow, eagerly anticipating this day. I could not get enough of you. I came into your dreams."

"Nightmares," she said, correcting him. Always she had had the same dream of shadows covering the moon, and then, like a specter, taking form and chasing her. "But why? What makes you want me when you could have anyone? There's nothing special about me." Her mind raced, picturing all the glamorous movie stars and wondering why it hadn't chosen one of them instead.

"When Stanton trapped you in his memory, he took you back in time, and I was able to witness your bravery before you were even born. The fierceness in your attempt to rescue Stanton when he was a boy impressed me. How could I not want you after I saw your willingness to sacrifice yourself for a child you didn't even know?"

"For my act of kindness, I'm condemned for eternity." She shambled back, hoping to get away from the Atrox, if only for a moment, so she could breathe air that wasn't tainted with its evil.

The Atrox tightened its hold on her and went on. "After I saw you, I went to the Moirai and asked them to let me become your soul's guardian."

"So I didn't choose you!" she shouted rebelliously. "I didn't. I knew I couldn't have."

"You didn't refuse me, either," it answered, undaunted. "The dark of the moon has always had a strange hold on you. You thought it was because Daughters are weakest then, but those nights of darkness awakened something deep inside you: something you feared, because even then, you sensed me waiting in your future."

She heard the scuffling of feet, and hope rose inside her.

The Atrox suddenly drew back.

She took in a deep breath, then gasped for more air, filling her starved lungs.

For a moment she thought Catty and Stanton had returned. Instead, three women entered the room. Vanessa knew at once that they were the Moirai, the three sisters of Fate.

The oldest one carried a pair of shears encrusted with blood.

Vanessa assumed she was Atropos: the one who cut the thread of life at the time of death.

"Is this the one?" she asked, studying Vanessa.

The youngest carried colored threads and wore a spindle that hung from a rope tied around her waist. She was definitely Klotho.

The one in the middle, who stood the tallest and carried herself as if she were the one in charge, was Lachesis. Her long fingers moved restlessly, seeming to push an invisible shuttle back and forth.

"We've come to witness the fulfilling of our decree and have our revenge against Selene," Atropos said.

"Selene favors you," Lachesis said, walking around Vanessa and looking her up and down. "But I don't see anything extraordinary about you."

"And where is the bravery that the Atrox wants to possess?" Klotho asked, examining Vanessa's face. "I see only tears in her eyes, not fierce determination."

"She's trembling," Atropos added. "She doesn't look very brave to me."

"Change my fate," Vanessa demanded.

The three sisters paused and then burst into laughter.

"Our decree is immutable," Atropos answered proudly.

"I was with you at the moment of your birth," Klotho said. "I spun your thread of life from my spindle." She pulled more threads from her pocket. "These are souls waiting to be born, ordinary lives. If only you could have seen your thread. It was magnificent. The finest I've ever made. I gave it to Lachesis."

"I wove the darkness into your life," Lachesis said proudly. "I'm the Disposer of Lots, the one who gave you your destiny."

"That I'll become a Follower," Vanessa muttered angrily.

"First, you will fall everlastingly in love with the Atrox," Lachesis said, appearing to take pleasure in what she was saying. "After all, I needed a reason for you to become a fallen goddess, and that is the best one."

Vanessa was stunned. "But the Atrox can't feel love."

"Nevertheless, you will be drawn to it and spend an eternity trying to make it love you," Lachesis explained. "And, in your quest to win its love, you'll forsake your goddess role and bring untold sorrows to the world as you try desperately to please it."

"I can't love it," Vanessa said.

"But you will," Lachesis countered. "Unrequited love is my favorite curse to give a human: to let them love and not have their love returned. How they wrestle with that one!"

"The sleepless nights . . ." Klotho interjected.

"Sometimes I cut their life threads early just to end their foolish misery." Atropos snapped her shears, the blades dangerously close to Vanessa's face. She leaned back away from the point.

"I can't fall in love with a shadow," Vanessa

said, determined to fight the fortune that they had given her.

"It's your destiny," Lachesis said. "You have no choice."

"I won't accept it," Vanessa said belligerently. "We make our own futures."

"Your future is with me," the Atrox said and wound itself tightly around her again.

Vanessa closed her eyes, unable to bear its touch.

"O Mater Luna, Regina nocis, adiuvo me nunc." The prayer was spoken only in times of grave danger, but Vanessa supposed it worked, as well, when the future looked hopeless.

"I will not have that prayer spoken in my presence!" The Atrox ripped away the chain holding her moon amulet and spun from her in fury.

Vanessa had been clutching her charm with both hands the entire time. Now, defeated and forsaken, she let it go. It hit the floor with a loud clunk, its magic luster gone. She stared down at a small black stone.

The amulet was a symbol of her real power,

her faith in her ability to turn evil away, but she had no confidence left. She closed her eyes and let her hands fall down to her sides. She was ready to receive her fate.

Cold fingers touched her chest, poking and prodding at her.

She opened her eyes.

"Who wove this destiny?" Klotho asked, thumping her knuckles against the tattoo on Vanessa's chest.

"I did it," Vanessa answered, trying to push their hands away. "It matches a design I made with flames in a ceremony."

"It overrides the destiny we gave her," Lachesis said, after studying it. "This one fates her to save the world, not destroy it."

"Selene!" Atropos touched the tattoo with the tip of her shears. A shiver raced through Vanessa. "Selene defied us again."

"Selene didn't do it," Vanessa protested. "I did it."

Lachesis narrowed her gaze. "During a ceremony in moonlight, no doubt," she said, with utter contempt. "I hate the moon. How can it give people hope in the middle of the disasters and tragedies that I weave into their lives?"

"Selene won't override us this time." Klotho pinched Vanessa's chest.

"Ouch!" Vanessa took a quick step back, but Klotho didn't let go. She tugged and pulled out the tip of a black thread from beneath Vanessa's skin. As she continued to pull, the lines of Vanessa's tattoo unraveled until finally a long thread dangled between Klotho's fingers.

Vanessa reached for it, but Klotho was faster. She handed it to Atropos.

"We've waited for centuries to have our revenge," Atropos said. "No one will stop us from having this moment." She grinned. "A dead person has no fate, and the death of this one here will inflict terrible pain on Selene."

"I want to see her cry," Lachesis said with glee.

"She'll grieve," Klotho whispered happily.

Vanessa watched in horror as Atropos placed the thread between the blades of her shears.

CHAPTER TWENTY-TWO

THE ATROX HOVERED above them, rumbling angrily. Vanessa wondered if it planned to rescue her from the Fates.

"Even Zeus, the king of the gods, must bow to our decree," Klotho said, quieting the Atrox. "Atropos is the inevitable that all humans must face. No one can stop her, not even the Atrox."

Atropos sniggered, then closed the shears. The sharp edges didn't cut the thread. She grinned unpleasantly and gritted her teeth as her thumb and fingers worked the handles up and down. The blades closed and opened with furious repetition until the hinge pin broke and the shanks fell apart. Atropos looked down at her ruined shears.

"Selene!" she screamed, spewing spittle over Vanessa's face.

"Her power is stronger!" Vanessa yelled joyously.

Lachesis smiled wickedly. She took the thread in her hands and stretched it.

Her sisters leaned closer to watch.

With artistry and skill, Lachesis tied the thread, looping it around and over into a delicate pattern that resembled the knots in the macramé plant hangers on Vanessa's patio at home.

"Amazing," Klotho purred.

"Selene isn't as wise as she thinks," Atropos added.

When Lachesis finished, she handed the knotted thread to Vanessa. "I've woven a new destiny for you," Lachesis said.

Vanessa waited to hear what she had been condemned to endure this time.

"You will express the evil that lies dormant inside you: *all* of its horrible destruction," Lachesis said with assurance. "That is my final decree, and it is immutable. Selene can't rescue you now."

The Atrox murmured its satisfaction.

After that, the Fates stomped away, their skirts rustling over the floor. Klotho grabbed her spindle and hit it against the wall. Stones grated against each other as the passage opened. The three sisters hurried out into a hallway.

Vanessa saw her chance and sprinted after them, but as she tried to duck out with them, Klotho spun around.

"You're destiny is here." She pressed her palm over Vanessa's face and pushed her back.

Vanessa stumbled and started to fall. The Atrox caught her before she hit the floor. Then it coiled around her with sensual slowness and helped her stand up.

"Your true allegiance is to me," it said.

"No. That's not true." Vanessa began to draw back in disgust, but the Atrox had already engulfed her. In spite of her terror, she wasn't going to surrender without a fight. Courage grew inside her. "I fought you once alone," Vanessa said.

"You didn't win," it cooed. "I let you escape."

She roused herself and pictured the full moon, hoping its image would give her strength, but the Atrox seeped into her mind and muddled her thoughts. Its evil swirled inside her, seducing her and awakening the darker spirit that had always lived within her.

"Please, stop," she implored, but she was too late. She was drowning in its evil. Still, the feeling wasn't as horrible as she had imagined.

"Vanessa," the Atrox said. "Your future lies with me. Consider carefully what that means." The silky command in its voice made her stop struggling.

"Imagine if you were all-powerful." The Atrox had found her frustration with Corrine, and it pulled those memories to the front of

Vanessa's mind. "You could have revenge for all the hurts you've had to endure."

Did she want revenge? She hadn't thought so until this moment. The answer surprised her. Corrine wasn't the only one who had hurt her feelings. There were others in the past. How precious her satisfaction would be to see them wounded in repayment for all her injuries.

The Atrox sensed her weakening. "You can have your revenge for all the insults you were forced to ignore. Remember the times you had to pretend not to hear rude comments because you wanted to be polite and not get into an argument?"

"But why did they say such things?" she asked, seeing her memories from a different angle now.

"Because they knew you were too nice to strike back," the Atrox whispered.

Anger rose inside her. The force of it surprised her. "I hate being nice," she said.

"The price is too high," the Atrox agreed. "I can feel your desire to be with me now. Let me show you the world in ways you've only imagined it before. You don't need to follow the rules and live a lackluster life. Indulge in your new destiny. You've struggled long enough, and you've lost everyone. Let me be your new family."

Something inside her collapsed. She gave up the struggle and turned slowly, looking at the darkness surrounding her. She wished she could see a face.

"I can't materialize," the Atrox said, "but maybe this will do." It pulled itself together, and a phantom appeared. She gazed into its ghostly features, and in her mind's eye she saw a handsome man, someone she could love.

"I can feel your desire to be with me," it whispered.

A sweet, bitter taste filled her mouth. Had it kissed her?

The phantom-form pulled her closer. Its arms wrapped around her, then grew into terrible dark wings that enfolded her.

"My guardian," Vanessa murmured. The Atrox had always been with her.

"Love me," the Atrox cooed.

"Yes," she whispered.

CHAPTER TWENTY-THREE

VANESSA LEANED BACK, waiting for the Atrox to kiss her again, but someone ripped her away from her phantom lover. She screamed her outrage and fought against the arms holding her. She had a violent, uncontrollable need to be back in the embrace of her beloved Atrox.

"Vanessa," someone repeated her name and patted her back, trying to mollify her.

But she didn't want anyone to calm her down. She longed for the Atrox. Only its shadow gliding over her could soothe her. She fought the arms restraining her and tried to pry herself free.

"Let me go!" she screamed, and then another voice made her stop. She listened.

Catty was speaking in Latin, but after she finished an invocation, she began saying words in a much older language, one that Vanessa didn't understand. Even so, there was something familiar about the chant. The cadence of the words sounded dangerously close to that of a prayer.

The Atrox roared.

Vanessa tugged and labored against the arms holding her until she could turn enough to see the Atrox. Its spectral face was miserably contorted. What was Catty doing to it?

"Stop!" Vanessa screamed. "You're hurting it."

The phantom stretched and extended itself in ever-increasing size until it became a thick black cloud against the ceiling.

Vanessa cried out, longing to hold it.

Catty walked beneath the churning darkness

and lifted her arms in supplication. But Vanessa knew Catty wasn't praying to the Atrox. She was summoning other powers to destroy it. Catty had started on the Path written in the Secret Scroll, and Vanessa had to stop her.

The Atrox screamed. Its shadow twitched and quivered, frantically trying to escape the room. But whatever power Catty had summoned was greater.

Vanessa needed to free the Atrox. She looked up to see who was restraining her. Stanton glanced back at her. She smirked and stopped struggling. She could trick him easily with a lie. She curled her lips into her nicest girlie smile.

"Thank you for saving me," she fibbed.

"I'm glad you're okay," he answered.

His hold loosened, just as she knew it would. She seized the opportunity, and, with a sudden violent twist, wiggled free; then she raced across the bedroom with only one goal in mind: to stop Catty.

Vanessa thrust her body forward, eager to slam Catty against the wall.

A hand whacked her back. Vanessa stumbled and fell to the floor. She hit her chin and bit her tongue. Blood filled her mouth. She rolled over and groaned.

Stanton lifted her to her feet.

Her mind felt muddled; her head throbbed. "Why was I trying to hurt Catty?" she asked.

"The Atrox was making you do it." Stanton held her tightly but this time she didn't want him to let her go. She needed his comfort. Tears ran down her cheeks and soaked into his shirt.

"Sorry," Stanton whispered, brushing the blood from her lips with the tail of his shirt. "I didn't mean to hurt you, but I had to break the trance that the Atrox had put over you. It was trying to use you to stop Catty."

"Trance?" Vanessa's thoughts were still unclear, and her back ached. She became aware of the peculiar taste mixing with the blood in her mouth. At the same time, a blurred memory that made her want to retch came into her mind.

"Please tell me I didn't kiss the Atrox," she said.

"You fell hopelessly in love with it," Stanton said. "Its powers are amazing."

Vanessa cringed. "You really did use me as bait to catch it."

"Catty and I had to deceive you," Stanton answered. "If we told you our plan, the Atrox would have found it in your mind, and then we wouldn't have been able to catch it by surprise."

A sob choked her as she imagined spending eternity with the Atrox and doing its bidding in futile attempts to win its love.

"It couldn't love me back," she said at last, "but that was never going to stop me from trying to win its affection." She thought of the three sister Fates. The first destiny that they had woven for her had almost come true.

"Catty knew her plan was dangerous," Stanton said. "She was worried we wouldn't be able to pull you back out of the trance."

Vanessa tried to turn to see Catty, but Stanton held her too tightly.

"Let me see her," Vanessa ordered, suddenly worried.

Catty had stopped praying.

"What is she doing now?" Vanessa asked.

And then Catty's voice sounded clear and pure as she yelled, "I will annihilate the evil before me!"

"She's quoting from the Secret Scroll," Stanton said.

Overhead, the Atrox jerked and thrashed, trying to escape the invisible force that held it and made it decrease in size.

"We need to help Catty," Vanessa said, with rising urgency. "She can't fight the Atrox alone."

In answer, Stanton pressed Vanessa against him and held her head down so she couldn't look back. "Catty doesn't want you to see," he said.

"What?" Vanessa asked, near panic. "What doesn't she want me to see?"

"It was her last wish that—" Stanton began.

"What do you mean, *last wish*?" Vanessa tried to pull away.

"She wants you to remember her the way she was," Stanton said.

"Let me see her," Vanessa said. "We can't let

her fight the Atrox alone. You have to let me help her."

"You can't," Stanton answered. "She's the Destroyer. It has always been her destiny to face the Atrox alone. She's known this for a long time."

"Did she remember to bring the black diamond?" Vanessa asked, trying to quell the panic rising inside her. "Catty is always so rash and impetuous. If she forgot it, she'll attack the Atrox anyway."

"Haven't you figured it out yet?" Stanton asked, stroking her hair. "Catty *is* the black diamond."

Vanessa froze.

"Her given name is Atertra," Stanton explained. "Her mother named her that, because it means 'unlucky.' She knew Catty was destined to become the heir to the Secret Scroll. But Atertra also means 'black,' and her father's last name, Adamantis, stands for many things, including 'diamond.'"

"There is no gem that fell from the Atrox's crown?" Vanessa asked. "No wish-granting diamond?"

"Catty told me that her father thought it was funny to spread the stories about the black diamond," Stanton went on. "He told everyone that it had power over all the magic in the universe. He loved to watch the pandemonium his rumors created among the Followers and the false hope his stories gave to the *servi*."

Stanton pulled Vanessa back to the farthest corner of the room. Immediately, she knew he was trying to protect her from what was going to happen next. She listened to Catty. She had been incanting prayers again, and now she stopped.

"My power is uncompromising and direct!" Catty shouted. "I am the Destroyer."

The Atrox screamed with a hellish sound that made Vanessa shudder.

"I am the absolute force of the divine," Catty said.

The floor began to tremble. The vibration quivered up Vanessa's legs. She strained to see her friend, and when she peered around, she gasped. The Atrox's shadow had become a sphere that now split open, inviting Catty into its center.

Catty stepped forward.

"I can't lose her again." Vanessa struggled against Stanton.

"You can't follow her," Stanton argued.

Vanessa bit his hand, surprising him, and then wrenched free. She ran into the shadow after Catty. The Atrox's power throbbed through her and made her afraid, but another force, something pure and good, and far more powerful than that of the Atrox, vibrated in the air and filled her with awe.

Catty stood in the middle of the swirling mass, her hair whipping around her. A silver aura pulsed over her.

"Leave the shadow," Catty ordered. She stared at Vanessa with an intensity that Vanessa had never seen in her eyes before. "I don't want you to get hurt," Catty warned, "but I can't stop for you, either."

Catty fixed her attention back on the shadows rolling ominously above her, inches from the top of her head. Its rumbling hurt Vanessa's ears.

"The Scroll's energy is inside me," Catty

explained. "I've always understood what my sacrifice would be."

"Please," Vanessa said. "We'll find another way."

"There *is* no other path," Catty said. Her gaze fixed on the darkness above her.

"Dingirmah!" Catty shouted. Her body shimmered with light.

Vanessa didn't know what the word meant, but she could feel its immeasurable energy. The sound echoed through her chest. Her heart lurched and skipped a beat.

The Atrox howled mournfully. Its shadow continued to contract until it was as thick as coal tar, pressing down heavily on her.

Vanessa couldn't breathe. She stumbled back. She needed to see what Catty was going to do.

Catty lifted her arms and yelled. *"Nimena!"*

The word became a force, calling on the One. The sound thundered and rocked the ground. Vanessa fell to the floor. She could feel Stanton's hands on her shoulders, trying to pull her back, but she remained inside the darkness, watching Catty.

Before the reverberation of the last word had ended, Catty called out the name of the creator of the universe, a word too sacred to be spoken. She invoked it anyway.

The Atrox screamed in agony and continued to compress and squeeze around Catty, but she didn't falter. Her lips continued moving in prayer, her light absorbing the Atrox's darkness.

Vanessa felt the immense power that had come into the room. She knew she was standing in the presence of the divine, the sacred One. The pressure continued to build.

Finally, unable to endure the energy anymore, Vanessa scrambled out of the darkness and into Stanton's arms. He held her tightly against him. She glanced back.

The Atrox vanished, and Catty disappeared with it.

CHAPTER TWENTY-FOUR

VANESSA FELL TO her knees and stared at the place where Catty had been moments before. An odd, sick wanting filled her chest.

"The prophecy is fulfilled," Stanton whispered reverently.

"I should have known she'd never betray the Daughters." Vanessa struggled to speak. Her voice was strangely high-pitched and thin, her throat too tight. "The Secret Scroll can only be given to someone who has a pure heart and the strength to fight the Atrox. Why did I ever doubt her?"

Stanton let Vanessa have a moment of silence. Then he touched her shoulder sympathetically. "Try to be happy for her."

Vanessa looked up, surprised. If that was supposed to comfort her, it didn't. How could she feel happy about anything with Catty gone?

"Chris promised Catty that they would be together again after the Atrox was defeated," Stanton said, "but he never explained how. Maybe this is what he meant."

Vanessa imagined Catty and Chris, two spirits frolicking together, but the image of them in paradise did not console her. She wanted Catty with her, not in some blissful hereafter.

"We need to find Serena," Stanton said gently. He took her hand and tried to make her stand up.

"I can't move," Vanessa replied. Her sadness felt too heavy. Grief pressed down on her physically, a burden she could not bear. "I don't have enough energy. Go without me."

Stanton pulled her up to her feet. "I can't leave you behind. A Regulator or a Follower might find you."

She leaned against him, and he cradled her in his arms. His tenderness made tears flow from her eyes but she had no other sensation of crying.

His body dissolved, and her hands started to blur. He was forcing her to go with him.

When she became transparent, Stanton guided her, taking her with him. They slipped under the stones in the hidden passage and breezed through the castle, then plunged together from a window and sped between the tall, narrow houses.

Shape-shifting Followers darkened the sky. The ghostly shadows swelled and bulged as the wind currents changed. The streets were jammed with dark shapes flying in all directions. The Followers seemed to sense that the Atrox had been destroyed and were rushing hectically around.

Regulators had stopped patrolling the streets. Instead of tromping back and forth, they had gathered on corners, their monstrous faces confused and morose.

Vanessa wondered what they would do without the Atrox to guide them, but she held that thought only for a moment. She had sensed Stanton's urgency, and now she understood it. They needed to find Serena. She was the key: the only one with the power to close the boundaries between the two worlds and stop the Followers from leaving Nefandus and invading Earth.

Stanton and Vanessa materialized inside the palace where she had been imprisoned with Serena. Vanessa ran through the suite of rooms and came back to Stanton. "She's not here."

Stanton stood completely still, his gaze intense. The room filled with a barely audible hum as his energy grew and he searched with his mental vision for Serena.

At last he blinked. His body relaxed, but his scowl didn't go away. He clenched his teeth.

"Is she all right?" Vanessa asked nervously. "Please tell me that she is. I can't lose another friend."

"Adamantis is using her to bring me to him," Stanton said grimly. "Without the Atrox, I'm the only one who stands in the way of his ruling Nefandus. He wants to destroy me." He grabbed Vanessa's hand, and instantaneously they were shadows again, spinning out the window. Their spectral forms raced past a row of lanterns set in a wrought-iron railing, and then they skimmed over the flagstone path that led to an austere mansion.

"Adamantis lives here," Stanton said as they materialized again on the veranda.

Vanessa had gone there once with Catty. That time, they had entered through a basement window. "Catty must have felt miserable living in this house," Vanessa said. "There's nothing warm or cozy about it."

Unexpectedly, grief hit her again, a surprise attack that made her chin quiver. "I wish I had been a better friend. She tried to tell me how horrible her life had been in Nefandus, but at the time I was too wrapped up in my own pain to really listen to her."

Stanton embraced her. "Catty understood," he said. "I know she did."

Without warning, flames shot from the mouths of the jade dragons on either side of the door. The firelight danced over the stained-glass panels. The devils depicted within the mosaic of colored glass turned. Their fierce stares made Vanessa take a step back. She had a feeling that they were telling Adamantis who was at the door.

"Your theatrics annoy me, Adamantis." Stanton punched his fist through the window.

Instead of falling, the broken glass spun out and whirled around them. Vanessa screamed and threw her arms up to protect her eyes. The glass scattered and finally fell to the porch. Vanessa rubbed at the tiny nicks stinging her forehead and arms.

The door opened. Vanessa peered inside. No one stood in the entrance to welcome them.

Stanton walked in. "I think Adamantis is expecting us."

Hesitantly, Vanessa followed him. As soon as she stepped over the threshold, cello music filled the air.

"Serena!" Vanessa screamed, anxious to see her friend. She raced toward the melodic sound. Maybe Serena was playing so joyfully because she knew the Atrox had been destroyed. Vanessa charged into the room at the far end of the hallway and stopped dead.

Adamantis held a cello between his legs and was sliding the bow feverishly across the strings. His thin hair had fallen into his eyes. He looked up and grinned victoriously. Vanessa knew he was enjoying the disappointment he saw on her face.

"Aren't you going to applaud my performance?" he asked.

"I hate you," Vanessa answered.

"Were you expecting someone else?" he added with a self-satisfied smile.

He tossed the bow across the room. It clattered noisily, then came to rest near the fireplace. Flames shot out greedily, trying to grasp the kindling and pull it into the fire.

"Where's Serena?" Vanessa asked.

"Why do you think she's here?" Adamantis gave the cello to the flames. The fire howled and raced around the instrument, devouring it. Black smoke curled up and seeped over the mantelpiece, leaving a trail of black soot on the white marble.

"I know you have her," Vanessa said defiantly.

His hard, dour expression frightened her. She eased back.

"I don't want to waste more time with you," he said impatiently. "Where is Stanton? He's the only one who could have located Serena here, so I know he's nearby, and I need to speak to him."

Vanessa didn't answer. She surveyed the room, searching for Serena. Then she found her, sitting on a stool in the farthest corner. Her eyes had a spellbound stare that made Vanessa shudder.

"Serena!" Vanessa ran to her.

"She can't hear you," Adamantis said, clearly vexed. "Tell me what happened to Stanton. I know he's here someplace."

"Find him with your mental vision if you're so powerful and need to see him," Vanessa snipped. She ignored Adamantis, fuming angrily behind her, and hugged Serena.

"Don't leave me," she whispered into Serena's ear. "I couldn't bear to lose you, too."

Serena looked pale and weak. The first time Vanessa ever saw her, her hair had been short and colored Crayola red, the strands twisted into bobby-pin curls. She had worn garish purple lipstick and red-brown shadow around her green eyes. The memory made Vanessa smile and hug her again.

"We'll go back to Los Angeles and dye our hair electric blue," Vanessa said into Serena's ear. "We'll escape this. I promise. Just hang on."

Adamantis grabbed her by the shoulder and yanked her away from Serena. "Get Stanton," he ordered.

"Don't touch me." Vanessa jerked back and slapped his hand away. "You sacrificed Catty," she accused bitterly. "From the moment she was born, that's what you had planned: to let her die fighting the Atrox."

Adamantis waved his hand dismissively. "Catty knew what would happen to her. It was her choice."

"You have no shame," Vanessa said, amazed. "None at all." She felt sickened by the depth of his depravity. And, at the same time, she felt sorry for him, because he was unable to feel love.

Adamantis glowered at her, and from his look she knew that he had read her thoughts about him. "Don't pity me," he snarled. "Your sympathy is wasted. I suppose Catty meant so much to you that you would have stopped her, had you known."

"That's what friends do," Vanessa said. "She and I would have found another way to destroy the Atrox."

"You're a fool." The cruelty in his expression made her think of Catty again. Tears welled up in her eyes. "Poor Catty," she whispered thinly.

Adamantis regarded her with utter disdain. "Why would the goddess Selene have ever chosen you? You have nothing goddess about you, and without the Atrox to back you, even the darkness that the Fates gave you is pathetically weak."

Vanessa shrank back. What little self-esteem she had left was gone now. She supposed that was the power of evil. It could steal your confidence and your belief in yourself, suck everything from you, until you felt unsure and too afraid to fight back.

At last, Stanton walked into the room. Vanessa wondered what he had been doing that had made him linger in the hallway for so long. Maybe he had been building his courage to face Adamantis.

"I'm so glad to see you, Stanton," Adamantis said gleefully. "The Atrox is destroyed. That leaves only you in my way."

"You want to fight me?" Stanton asked. "Is that what this is about?"

"Fight you?" Adamantis answered. "Never. You'd surely win."

Stanton looked confused. He glanced at Serena. "Then why . . . ?"

"I have a far more interesting way to destroy you," Adamantis announced.

Stanton looked confused.

"You still feel love," Adamantis said with jubilation.

"What would make you think that?" Stanton asked. "I'm a Follower, the Prince of Night. I can't love."

"Catty believed she was deceiving me," Adamantis went on. "I let her think she had, of course, because that gave me time to wander about her mind and visit all her memories. You can't imagine my surprise when I discovered memories of you with Serena." He studied Stanton. "The Prince of Night still feels love. After I realized this was true, I went along with your deception as well, because I knew I could use your secret to my advantage one day."

"Like now," Stanton said.

"Precisely," Adamantis replied. "This love of yours is so deep, so fervent and passionate, that it makes you risk your own existence time and again in order to ensure Serena's safety."

Stanton didn't reply.

"Would you do it again for me?" Adamantis stepped back to Serena, and before Vanessa could stop him, he slashed the blade of a slender knife across her throat. Blood trickled from the cut and ran in tiny streams down her skin.

Stanton did nothing, but the anguish in his eyes revealed his feelings.

"Serena is mortal," Adamantis continued, obviously deriving pleasure from Stanton's pain. "She can die. Life is so fragile for humans, but an Immortal is harder to destroy, especially the Prince of Night. Still, I'm told that anyone who loves as deeply as you do will surrender their own life to save their beloved. Is that true? Would you kill yourself to save Serena?" He held his knife poised in the air near Serena's eye.

"Yes," Stanton answered without any emotion.

"Ah," Adamantis sighed in an expression of satisfaction. "What a wonderful event this will be."

A Regulator stomped into the room and gave Vanessa a snaky grin. She immediately understood what Adamantis wanted Stanton to do. Catty had described the way Regulators destroyed Immortals when she told Vanessa how Kyle and his friends had been executed.

"You can't trust Adamantis," Vanessa warned.

"You don't know that he'll release Serena from the trance."

She suddenly realized how much she cared for Stanton, in spite of all the times she had thought that he had betrayed her. They had become close friends. The first time he pulled her into his memories, she had seen his struggle. She had watched him as a small boy hug his grandfather's tombstone. She had experienced his loneliness and knew how hard he had fought the evil inside him when he became an *invitus*; taken by the Atrox and forced to become a Follower against his will. He had become the Prince of Night only because he needed the power to save Serena. Vanessa rushed over to Stanton and grabbed his arm, trying to hold him back.

"I can't let anything happen to Serena." Stanton pulled away from her and started toward the Regulator. "She has the power to close the boundaries. The Atrox was the only force that kept her from sealing them before. Tell her to do so immediately. She needs to stop the Followers who are escaping Nefandus. They'll become a deadly menace to the people in Los Angeles."

As he spoke, prismatic lights began floating around Serena. Then an ethereal brightness covered her. Vanessa wondered if Adamantis had done something to her, but he was focused on Stanton, eagerly anticipating his execution.

The Regulator pounded his chest and spread out his arms, waiting for Stanton.

Vanessa stared angrily at Adamantis. Lachesis had said that Vanessa was destined to express the evil that lay dormant inside her. Did she dare use it now to save Stanton? The Atrox had told her that she alone could ensure the final eclipse. So she must have huge power inside her. Even Selene had told her that she did. That force might have been intended for evil, but it was her decision as to whether she used it for good or bad.

"I won't let you do this to Stanton," she said finally.

"Nefandus has no moon," Adamantis laughed, seeming to delight in her misery. "Your nice little goddess powers won't work here."

"The Fates gave darkness to my soul," she

said. "You were once afraid of it. That's why you wanted me dead."

"*If* you had become a fallen goddess," he said, unimpressed by her challenge. "But without the Atrox, you're weak."

She did not let his words defeat her this time. "You were terrified of what I could become," she challenged. She lifted her hand, releasing a slender stream of what she kept locked deep inside. It unfurled, and the air vibrated ominously.

"Does the goddess hope to scare me with a display of fireworks?" Adamantis stopped the Regulator from grabbing Stanton. "Let me get rid of the goddess first. I don't want any distractions while I watch the Prince dissolve." Then he spoke to Vanessa: "Are you foolish enough to think you can fight me and win?"

He didn't wait for her reply, but sent out a force that wrapped around her. It continued tightening until she couldn't breathe. She closed her eyes and endured the pain; she refused to surrender.

The air around her felt impossibly hot. With a start, she realized that the heat was coming from her energy. She could feel the fire burning inside her. Her rage and anger made her dizzy. This was her evil power. These were her negative emotions, the ones she tried to contain. Those energies could be malicious and used to do foul things, but they also had the power to protect her.

When she opened her eyes again, Adamantis lifted his hand with the threat of another assault.

Vanessa did not cower. She held her hand up and blocked his second attack. It burst apart and hit the ceiling and walls. Plaster crumbled and rained over them.

Stanton jumped away from the Regulator and joined her. "Good work," he whispered. He braced his hands against her shoulders to steady her. Only then did she realize that the energy inside her was making her tremble.

She glared at Adamantis and released her power. "This is for Catty," she said quietly, "because you couldn't love her and see how precious she was."

The violent force threw Adamantis back against the wall.

Stanton hugged her. "I didn't know you

could be such a hellcat," he said joyously.

"That was my evil side," Vanessa answered, smiling crazily. "I wished I'd known that fighting back could feel so good."

"You stood up for yourself," Stanton said, "and for me and Serena."

She nodded. The second destiny that Lachesis had woven for her had come true. She had used the power that was deep inside her, the full horrible force of it. She had beaten Adamantis. So why was he smiling triumphantly?

"You can have Nefandus," he said as he held out his arm and let his Regulator help him stand. "The earth realm will be my new dynasty." He started to dissolve. "Maybe I'll marry your mother, Vanessa." He laughed heartily.

She took aim at him again, but he had already turned into a black smudge that whipped around the mantel, flitted over the fire, and disappeared up the chimney.

The Regulator howled, abandoned and afraid. Then, whimpering, he faded and raced after Adamantis.

The room became still.

Stanton ran to Serena. He tenderly placed his arms around her and held her against him. Then he stared into her eyes. Vanessa knew he was untangling the hypnotic state that Adamantis had placed her in.

When the trance lifted, Serena blinked and smiled.

Stanton kissed her forehead and let his lips linger before he pulled back and asked, "Did you close the boundaries?"

Serena nodded and brushed her hand over Stanton's cheek as she spoke, "They're closed." Her lips parted, and he kissed her lightly.

Stanton pulled her up and wrapped his arms around her. "I love you," he whispered against her cheek.

Reluctantly, he turned his attention back to Vanessa, without letting go of Serena. "As soon as you and I entered the house," Stanton explained, "I used my mental powers to find Serena and go into her mind."

"He dodged around all the barriers that

Adamantis put up," Serena continued as she gazed lovingly into Stanton's eyes. "And when he found me behind the trance, he told me that the Atrox had been destroyed and that I needed to seal the boundaries."

"I saw light glowing around you," Vanessa said.

"That was probably emanations from my power as I sealed the boundaries," Serena explained. "I couldn't have done it without Stanton." She leaned into him and rested her hands on his chest. "I've missed you," she whispered as she lifted her head for another kiss.

A terrible thought came to Vanessa.

"But if the portals are closing permanently, then how are we going to get back to Los Angeles?" She had a quick mental image of Adamantis when he threatened to marry her mother. Her stomach curdled. "We have to get back," she whispered, as new fear swept through her.

CHAPTER TWENTY-FIVE

STANTON CLASPED Vanessa's wrist. "I'll take you home," he said with calm assurance.

Vanessa closed her eyes and waited expectantly, but the veil never descended over her. Her eyes flashed open. They were still in the same room.

"Why isn't the passing working?" she said. Her anxiety was growing. Tension tightened her throat. "Do something. I have to go home."

Stanton appeared totally bewildered, his confidence faltering. He frowned and raked his fingers through his hair. "Let me try again." He wrapped his arms around the girls again and squeezed them tightly. His power buzzed through Vanessa.

But, again, nothing happened.

He dropped his hold on them and let his hands fall down to his sides. "My power doesn't work," he said with a look of stunned disbelief.

"Of course not," Serena said, panic rising in her voice. "I sealed the boundaries."

"I can't live here!" Vanessa screamed. For one heart-stopping moment she imagined spending the rest of her life in Nefandus. The thought made her ill. "How are we going to get home?"

"Your power worked more quickly than I thought possible," Stanton said to Serena, ignoring Vanessa's question. He gazed adoringly at Serena. "Your ability is awesome." He leaned down to kiss her.

"We don't have time for this," Vanessa squealed, cutting in on their embrace. "I want to go home and drive my car and eat candy that doesn't have an aftertaste of magic!" Her stomach clenched. "I can't bear to look at Regulators for the rest of my life."

"Let's try the portals." Serena wrested herself out of Stanton's arms. "If the portals were open when I sealed the boundaries, then they won't close permanently until the demon star becomes bright again. Is there a chance?"

"Where's the closest portal?" Vanessa shouted over her shoulder as she galloped toward the door. "I need to get home."

Serena ran after her, but before they reached the hallway, Stanton trapped them in his arms. He jammed them against his body as he turned into a shadow. His energy hummed around them and forced them to transform.

As soon as they were no more than murky silhouettes, he catapulted them out into the night with explosive speed.

Rain hammered through them. The downpour had driven the Followers and Regulators inside, and the streets below were empty.

As they materialized next to a street sign on the corner of Devil's Palm and Elk Horn, Vanessa realized that the tiny droplets pelting her weren't water but a thicker substance that felt sticky. It slid down the buildings, coating the roofs and gargoyles with a lustrous sheen. Here and there, red liquid gathered in puddles. The brilliance coming off the surfaces was blinding and gave the night a crimson glow.

"It's not a storm," Stanton explained, answering her thoughts. "Without the Atrox, the artificial sky is falling." He pointed to a pool of red that had flooded the street. "Even the fake stars have melted; what's left of them is falling to the ground."

Vanessa looked down and caught her breath. Red beads shimmered like dewdrops on her arms and outstretched hands. The cold from the Atrox's leftover magic seeped down to her bones but she didn't brush the droplets away. "How could something so evil create something so beautiful?" she wondered, awestruck.

Serena tugged at her. "We have to check the portal!"

Vanessa screamed, startled into action, and ran down the narrow alleyway. She splashed through the puddles of brightly shining red and fell against the wall. The bricks rippled, and her hands fell through.

"It's open!" she yelled exultantly, turning back to tell Serena, who was still standing with Stanton.

Any joy that Vanessa had felt left her when she saw the doleful expression on Stanton's face.

With a jolt, she realized that she was never going to see him again. She ran back and squeezed him tightly. A thousand words rushed through her head: things she had wanted to tell him and wished she had, but now had no time for.

"I should have told you so many things," she said hurriedly.

"I read every thought," he whispered, "even those that you repressed and kept hidden from yourself. I know. You don't have to say anything. Go home now."

"Thank you," she said simply.

He stared at Serena. "Stay with me."

"I can't," she answered too quickly.

He leaned down and gently placed a hand on either side of her face and held her still so that she was forced to look into his eyes. His fingers were trembling.

Vanessa sensed that he was opening his mind so that Serena could wander through his thoughts and see all his emotions.

When Serena stopped resisting and gazed into his eyes, Stanton said, with a worried hitch in his voice, "Everything I did, even turning back to the Atrox, was so I could be with you for eternity. I love you. Without you, my existence has no meaning. I need you."

The portal began shimmering.

"Make up your mind!" Vanessa screamed. "You've got to hurry!" She stepped in and paused at the entrance. The portal bore down on her as it tried to close, but she remained there, waiting for Serena.

"I've been imprisoned way too long," Serena answered.

Stanton shook his head. "Don't tell me no."

"I want to see my world," Serena said. "I need to feel moonlight and play my cello."

"The moon will shine here by midnight," he said anxiously, "and I can give you a thousand cellos."

"Come with me," Serena said. "You can adjust to my world. You've lived there."

"My place is in Nefandus," Stanton answered. "Please, Serena, tell me you'll stay with me."

In answer, she slipped from his grasp.

He reached out and tried to catch her, but she dodged away from him and ran toward the portal. Her feet splashed wildly through the scarlet puddles.

In the lurid red light cast from the fallen stars, Vanessa could see the utter devastation on Stanton's face. Her heart went out to him.

"Stay and reign with me," he said desperately.

Without looking back, Serena took Vanessa's hand and stepped through the portal.

Stanton fell to his knees, despairing, and threw his head back. He screamed out his misery, and the sorrow in his cry made tears come to Vanessa's eyes.

CHAPTER TWENTY-SIX

STANTON'S SCREAM echoed around them. Vanessa could feel the despair in his voice, and she knew that Serena must be able to sense his anguish, too. Serena looked heartbroken, her eyes glassy with tears.

The portal started to close, but before the veil descended over them, Serena lifted her arm. A spear of light emanated from her fingertips and kept the portal open.

"They need me here, Vanessa," Serena said. "I hope you'll understand why I can't go back with you. I want to stay and help Stanton make Nefandus a world of light. As the key, I have that kind of power. I think that's why Selene gave me a third choice, so that I could become a goddess of the dark, like Hekate."

"It's the right decision," Vanessa said bravely even though her grief felt huge. Her chest tightened and she could barely breathe. She didn't want to lose another friend.

Serena hugged Vanessa with her free arm. "Try not to be sad. I love Stanton, and he truly makes me happy. I can't lose him, no matter what I have to sacrifice to stay with him."

Or what I have to sacrifice, Vanessa thought.

For Serena's sake, she tried to smile but her lips felt tight. Her left eye twitched nervously, and she knew her expression of joy for Serena was a grim imitation of delight.

"Our lives take too many twists and turns," Serena said, understanding Vanessa's distress. "Change is the only thing we can count on, and if we fight that, then we're fighting life."

Vanessa nodded. "Saying good-bye seems to be a big, bad chunk of it." She couldn't keep her tears from falling. She let them go as her chin quivered. She was blubbering. That wasn't the way she wanted Serena to remember her. She swallowed and choked back her sadness.

"We have to fulfill our destinies," Serena said, her voice faltering, "and we can't always take the people we love with us when we do." She embraced Vanessa again and kissed her cheek. Then she stepped out of the portal.

Before it closed, Vanessa pressed her face out and watched Serena run to Stanton.

Stanton jumped up, his expression hopeful, but uncertain.

"I love you, Stanton!" Serena told him. "Of course I'm going to stay with you."

He swept her into his arms and spun around, kissing her forehead, her temples, her cheeks. He was still spinning with her cradled in his arms when they dissolved into a shadow and spiraled away, a wispy plume of darkness in the crimson light.

Vanessa ducked back into the portal and tried to feel happy for them, but all she could do was count her own sorrows. The membrane covered her, and she became paralyzed as before.

Seconds later, dull pain rushed through her and awakened her senses. She stumbled forward and found herself standing in front of a fortune-teller's shop in Chinatown. Vanessa felt grateful to be back in L.A., but the sweetness of that feeling was tinged with a horrible longing for her friends.

The storefront windows were dark, the walkways deserted, the silence complete. She didn't know the time but suspected it must be very late. Her memories of everything that had happened, were still intact so she felt certain that she hadn't turned seventeen yet. She could still use her power to become invisible and catch a breeze home, but she didn't trust her emotions enough to try. She was too afraid of losing control and ending up in some faraway place like Albuquerque.

Moonlight silvered the undulating eaves of the pagoda-style buildings. She rushed down to the plaza, where the building wouldn't obscure her view. She stood beneath the paper lanterns that hung from the trees and smiled up at the moon.

Whatever had been eclipsing the lunar body had dissolved, and the moon's milky light cast a white glow over the night. But as she started to feel happy, another thought pressed down on her: the Atrox had lost, but at what price?

Slowly, she started walking home. She no longer had a moon amulet to warn her of danger, and with each step she cast worried glances at the shadows that seemed to be everywhere. Stanton had warned her that some Followers had been able to leave Nefandus before Serena could seal the boundaries. Surely, Adamantis had escaped into Vanessa's world.

As she hurried under a streetlight, a car slowed and pulled over to the curb. The window rolled down, and a girl leaned out. "Cool," the girl smiled. "What are you advertising?"

Vanessa didn't understand the question at first but then glanced down and saw that she was still covered with the residue of the fallen stars.

Her skin appeared sprinkled with sparkling red sequins.

"Great," she muttered to herself. "I'm part of a movie promo," she said to the girl.

Catty had used that same excuse a thousand times when she dropped out of the time tunnel into the wrong place and time. Vanessa pictured Catty's smiling face and became suddenly overwhelmingly frustrated. It wasn't right that Catty's sacrifice should go unnoticed.

She walked over to the car. "What do you think was blocking the moon?" she asked.

The girl glanced up at the sky. "Smoke from the fires. That's what the papers said. Why?"

"Would you believe me if I told you that an ancient evil called the Atrox was trying to destroy the moon?" Vanessa didn't wait for an answer. "The apparitions that everyone reported seeing were real. They weren't illusions caused by too much smoke in the air, but shape-shifters, who are Followers of the Atrox and have the power to transform into shadows and float through the night like ghosts."

"What made them go away, then?" the girl asked, wide-eyed. "The papers said the wildfires were finally put out."

"A goddess named Catty sacrificed her life," Vanessa explained. "She was a Daughter of the Moon who saved the world by destroying the Atrox."

The girl was quiet for a moment. Then she brightened. "Cool movie. I'll be sure to check it out."

The car pulled away.

Vanessa shook her head. No one would ever know the sacrifice that Catty had made to save the world, and that made her angry and sad. Her emotions mixed wildly. She looked up at the moon and yelled at Selene, "It's not fair!"

Screaming made her feel a little better. Starting off again at a brisk pace, she had almost reached the dragon archway when footsteps pounded on the sidewalk behind her.

As Vanessa started to turn to see who was trailing after her, a hand grabbed her shoulder. She was too exhausted and overwhelmed with grief even to cry out.

CHAPTER TWENTY-SEVEN

VANESSA HAD SMELLED Jimena's musk perfume before she turned completely around. She knew she was safe, but when she saw Jimena, sassy and clean in her white miniskirt, she didn't feel thankful or reassured. She had wanted an outpouring of sympathy from Jimena. Instead, she saw unmistakable joy on her face.

"Why are you so happy?" Vanessa snapped.

"You saved the world," Jimena said, brushing

back her silky hair. "Don't you want to celebrate?"

"Celebrate?" Vanessa couldn't tolerate Jimena's brisk cheerfulness. She felt her goddess power storming inside her, her anger rising.

"If you hadn't been brave enough to go back into Nefandus, then the destiny that the Fates decreed would have come true," Jimena explained. "Your show of bravery was your first step away from a terrible future and toward the good one woven in your tattoo."

"It's always a test, isn't it?" Vanessa retorted. "From the very first time Maggie told me that I couldn't rescue Catty. I'm sick of proving that I'm brave enough to be a Daughter. I never want to have anything to do with you or Selene again. You told me to hide, and Selene told me to have fun, but neither of you told me the truth."

Vanessa darted across the street, loosening her molecules, determined to get away from Jimena. She didn't care who saw her ghostly image. Let the scientists blame her apparition on lingering smoke or whatever excuse they wanted to use this time.

When she reached the curb, Jimena brushed her hand through Vanessa's transparent form. The touch made her molecules slam back together, and the impact caused her to lose her balance and totter. Jimena caught her. Vanessa shook her arm free and tried to stomp off, but Jimena hurried in front of her and blocked her way.

"Selene visited you because she was afraid I had been too convincing and that you wouldn't follow your heart," Jimena said. "She was worried that I had intimidated you, because you always follow the rules and do what you're told."

"You make that sound like a fault," Vanessa said.

"When you lose yourself in order to do what you think other people expect from you, then it is," Jimena said.

"It's not a problem that I have anymore," Vanessa said rudely.

Her turbulent emotions released the power that had been building inside her. It soared across the street and hit a billboard, starting a fire. Flames shot into the sky.

Vanessa turned threateningly to Jimena. "It's your fault Catty's gone," she said accusingly. "You should have told me the truth."

"I understand your anger," Jimena said, trying to console her.

"No, you don't," Vanessa snorted.

"I couldn't tell you that Catty was the black diamond," Jimena explained, no longer smiling. "If I had, you would have tried to find a way to save her, and that delay would have changed the final outcome. The Atrox would have won."

"You don't know," Vanessa argued. "Just leave me alone."

"I can't." Jimena gently touched Vanessa's shoulder. "Your birthday is today. You have to choose."

"Now?" Vanessa asked. "I need . . ." She suddenly understood her hostility. "I need time to mourn Catty, and if I make my choice, I'll lose my memories of what she did, of all the times . . . How can you make me choose now?"

"It's your seventeenth birthday," Jimena replied.

"I refuse," Vanessa said. "I'm not going to make a choice."

"You can't not choose."

"I just did," Vanessa said, feeling pleased with herself. "You can't make me choose."

Jimena followed silently behind Vanessa for a city block before she spoke again. "I've had time to mourn Catty," she said softly. "I knew what was going to happen. So I cried my tears already. I hate what happened, but I knew it was coming. It must have been a horrible shock for you."

Her sympathy surprised Vanessa, who stopped and faced her.

"And I knew Serena wouldn't be coming back," Jimena whispered. She took Vanessa's arm. "You've been through too much. And I was too excited that we had won. Of course you can't make your choice yet. Let me show you something."

Minutes later, they were in Jimena's car, speeding west down Wilshire Boulevard. Jimena didn't turn on the music, and the only sound came from the wind whipping through the open windows.

When they reached the beach, Jimena parked the car. They got out and strolled down to the shore. Moonlight cast pale magic across the sand. While they stood in the spumy edge of the surf, an irresistible impulse seized Vanessa and made her rush into the cold water. A wave slapped over her and washed away the red sparkles left from the stars. The crimson specks floated in the ocean and then, like bubbles, burst apart and disappeared.

Vanessa floated over the crest of a wave, then swam out beyond the breakers. She turned onto her back and drifted. The ocean current rocked her back and forth as the lunar glow worked on her.

Her molecules became restless, urging her to give in, to let go and float over the city one last time. Her skin began to twitch. Soon her arms were no more than moonlit specks, twinkling in the water.

She became invisible and rose toward the moon. Rays of alabaster light cleansed away her unpleasant anger. She relaxed and sailed aimlessly through the night.

Without warning, an air current whizzed past her. She bobbed in its wake and looked around. The stream of air returned and whooshed around her again and again until she was spinning.

"Catty?" Vanessa asked, expecting to hear her friend laugh.

The first time she had made Catty invisible, Catty had zoomed about the backyard, swooping down on Vanessa and buzzing over her head.

Vanessa couldn't see Catty at the moment, but then, she reasoned, no one standing on the shore could see Vanessa, either, and yet she was definitely there. Her spirits soared. She spun around and chased after the air current, but whatever had been there was gone.

She eased back to shore, materializing, a silver mist that trickled down and formed into a girl. When she was whole, she hugged Jimena.

"Thank you," she said, and then she added, "I'm sorry I was so angry."

Jimena held her close. "I know. I was angry, too, when I first found out. It still doesn't feel fair." She looked at her watch. "Did you decide?"

"I can't," Vanessa replied. "I have so many plans for college and a career. I want to travel and perform my music, but am I being selfish if I don't choose to become something more?"

"This is the most important decision of your life," Jimena said. "For once in your life, don't do what you think other people expect you to do."

"I want to be free of my goddess powers," Vanessa said quickly. "I want to be a regular girl." But then she remembered Catty's sacrifice. "Wait." She grabbed Jimena's arm. "Maybe I should do more."

She looked up at the night sky and wondered if Catty were waiting for her. She turned, hoping to see an unusual glimmer of light, something beckoning her to join it.

"You have only seconds to decide," Jimena warned.

Vanessa thought of her music. She had so many dreams about the songs she would write.

"I can't decide," she blurted. "My mind's all mixed up. Can't I have more time?"

"No!" Jimena insisted. "You have to make up your mind."

"Wait," Vanessa said. "One more thing."

Jimena's eyes widened in exasperation, and she anxiously pointed at her watch.

"Tell the new Daughters to use their gifts and enjoy them, because the time passes too quickly, and it's gone before you have a chance to realize how precious each moment is." Vanessa stopped. "There so much more I want to say."

"I know," Jimena said. "Now, choose."

Vanessa nodded, the beating of her heart thundering in her ears, and made her choice.

CHAPTER TWENTY-EIGHT

MICHAEL'S VOLKSWAGEN bus was parked in front of Vanessa's house. He jumped from the driver's seat when he saw her. He walked toward her and handed her a bouquet of red roses.

"Happy birthday," he said. "I was hoping you'd come home today. I've been waiting in my van since the sun set, just in case."

She felt a burst of joy. She loved the tousled, messy look of his new haircut, the way he was looking at her with such happiness. She pressed her face down into the flowers.

"Stanton talked to me the other night at Planet Bang," Michael said. "He told me that we should wait for moonlight and roses."

"Stanton?" Vanessa rubbed her temple. She remembered being with Michael outside Planet Bang when Stanton opened the van door. But she couldn't recall exactly what had happened after that. "I thought you didn't like Stanton."

"I was wrong about him," Michael went on. "He and I had a really long talk. You know what he told me?"

Vanessa shook her head.

"He told me that I should cherish you, because I would never know the sacrifice you've made to save the world." Michael laughed, but something felt true in what he said.

The words fluttered at the edge of Vanessa's thoughts, teasing her and not going away. She wished she could remember.

"He was a good friend." Vanessa looked away and wondered why she had called Stanton a friend when she hardly knew him.

"I know you want to see your mom," Michael said. "So I won't keep you." He kissed her forehead. "It's so great to have you back."

She watched him leave her.

"Stay home this time. Please!" he yelled as he darted around to the driver's side and jumped behind the steering wheel. The engine started with a roar. Michael waved as the van pulled away.

The front door opened, and Vanessa's mother raced toward her. "Vanessa!"

"Mom!" Vanessa shouted. She flung her arms out, throwing the flowers into the air, and ran to her mother.

Her mother embraced her and squeezed tightly, swaying back and forth. "Where have you been?" she asked between her kisses. "The detective handling your case said that you and Catty and Serena had run away. Is that true?"

A horrible emptiness filled Vanessa's chest. Her chin quivered, though she didn't understand